# ALICE'S AWAKENING

## Genevieve Lyons

Chivers Press • G.K. Hall & Co.
Bath, England   Thorndike, Maine USA

This Large Print edition is published by Chivers Press, England, and by G.K. Hall & Co., USA.

Published in 2000 in the U.K. by arrangement with Severn House Publishers Ltd.

Published in 2000 in the U.S. by arrangement with Chivers Press, Limited.

U.K. Hardcover ISBN 0-7540-4204-9  (Chivers Large Print)
U.K. Softcover   ISBN 0-7540-4205-7  (Camden Large Print)
U.S. Softcover   ISBN 0-7838-9109-1  (Nightingale Series Edition)

The text of this Large Print edition is unabridged.
Other aspects of the book may vary from the original edition.

Set in 16 pt. New Times Roman.

Printed in Great Britain on acid-free paper.

**British Library Cataloguing in Publication Data available**

**Library of Congress Cataloging-in-Publication Data**

Lyons, Genevieve.
   Alice's awakening / Genevieve Lyons.
      p.  cm.
   ISBN 0-7838-9109-1 (lg. print : sc : alk. paper)
   1. France, Southern—Fiction. 2. Fathers and daughters—
Fiction. 3. Journalists—Fiction. 4. Large type books.  I. Title.
PR6062.Y627 A79  2000
823'.914—dc21                                          00–039522

*This book is for
my enchanting god-daughter
Marissa Sackler with my love.*

# CHAPTER ONE

Alice Sandar turned slowly on her side. She could feel her pyjama bottoms twisting around her body as she moved and she pushed them down and sighed blissfully as she stretched her naked legs under the white covers on her bed. Shafts of light streaked her room like bars of gold but she kept her eyes firmly shut, savouring the last moments between sleep and wakefulness. She came slowly to life from her long sleep.

She had travelled from Spain the previous day and it had been a tiring journey. The drive through Andalucia was hot and dusty: ninety in the shade. Then there were the delays at the airport, fans fluttering all around her, though the place was air-conditioned. People were fretful and lethargic from the heat outside. By the time Alice reached France she was physically exhausted but blissfully happy to see her father waiting to meet her at Nice Airport. Kalo, the chauffeur and one of her father's bodyguards, waited with him just outside the baggage claim. She had seen her father's eyes light up and all her tiredness vanished. Everything was all right. Daddy was there! She had run into his welcoming arms, hugging him, kissing his cheek that smelled of cologne, whispering, 'Daddy, Daddy, Daddy. Oh, it's so good to be home.'

She had been emotionally worn out too, for she had said goodbye to the nuns in the convent school on that, her last day with them. She had graduated, her schooldays over, leaving the convent where she had been happy for good. She had bid them all, the girls and the nuns, a tearful farewell, promised to write, keep in touch, though deep down she knew that this was wishful thinking. They would all be scattered far and wide and though the nuns would remain *in situ*, nevertheless she was not likely to make that long journey once life had caught her up in its momentum.

Schooldays were over. Leaving the security and tranquillity of that place at the foot of the Sierras was exciting, challenging, but it was also quite frightening. She had been so protected there, so isolated from the rest of the world that it was quite a wrench to know she would never again be a pupil there, warmly surrounded by a discipline that guarded her and protected her from reality. The realisation that she was grown up now, that she would have to make decisions on her own, deal with life on life's terms was quite daunting. So while part of her was excited by the prospect of being an adult at last, the other part mourned the passing of her childhood, of irresponsibility, of dependence on others for almost everything.

She knew that her father, and mother to a

lesser degree, would be happy to assume the responsibility, take charge of her life, but she was determined not to allow them. She needed now, she admitted, albeit reluctantly, to make her own decisions, be independent, in charge.

So she had dined early with her parents on the terrace of their villa on Cap d'Antibes, gazing at the moon hanging like a huge silver lantern in the black velvet sky as the stars popped out one by one and the cicadas chattered in the thick greenery and the whisper of the sea lulled the senses.

Dinner was a quiet event—her mother and father never seemed to have much to say to each other—and Alice was very tired. By the time coffee was served she could hardly keep her eyes open and her mother suggested early bed.

Now, as the sunlight streaked through the shutters Alice threw back the covers and rose to a new dawn, a new life. Freedom beckoned. Life was about to happen. She hadn't the faintest idea what form it would take, but she would be ready.

Nana bustled into the room as Alice threw back the shutters.

'Oh it's lovely, lovely to be home,' she told Nana, stretching her arms.

Nana muttered something cryptic in reply. It was not her way to lavish praise on her charge. Excessive praise led to swollen heads and Nana, very firmly of the old school, believed there was nothing as unattractive as a swollen-headed miss. There were so many of them about these days, little madams strutting their stuff, half naked, flaunting pierced belly buttons and noses. But she had known Alice from a baby, and loved her to bits. Alice had just the right amount of decorum to satisfy Nana that she had done a good job.

'Now you get bathed and hurry down to breakfast, miss,' Nana instructed as if she was still six years old. Nana did not hold with showers. 'Places are missed, little crevices. No, there's nothing like a long soak in a tub as God meant.' How she knew what God meant was a mystery to all but Nana was quite certain she was *au fait* with his intent.

Alice sighed and looked out to where the azure sky met the cobalt sea. The air was warm and the waves were sprinkled with dancing lights glittering in the sun. Below her, on the terrace, beside the aquamarine swimming pool she could see her mother and father breakfasting. The top of her father's head was going bald, his silver hair a monklike tonsure, a frame for his head. She reflected how much she loved him but wondered apprehensively how he would deal with her grown up status. How much freedom would he permit her?

She went into the tiled bathroom off her bedroom and turned on the shower, adapting it to a medium temperature—when the maids cleaned each morning they always turned it to

4

cold. She showered, dressed, pulling on her jeans and tee shirt, disappointed that she did not feel any different today.

If Life with a capital L lay before her, this beginning was inauspicious. It seemed to her like any other day, first day of the holidays. She was eager for its mysteries to be revealed. She had dallied in the wings long enough; it was time to take centre stage, but how? When? The Spanish convent had shielded her from the thousand daily impacts most girls her age would have been exposed to almost anywhere else. Paris. Rome. New York. Oh, and most certainly, London. She had been protected by a Spanish society that still, even in the nineties, guarded its young females jealously. And Alice had been happy enough to be protected. Because deep down she knew there might be something fearful waiting for her.

Alice had been even more isolated in the convent, being English when most of the girls were Spanish, and she was nervous of being thrust into the hurly-burly of life. She knew, had always been aware that there was a secret at the heart of her family and part of her was terrified of finding out what it was. An inner voice which she dismissed as unrealistic warned her that the secret was malign, something she would not *want* to find out about. All her life there had been evasions, unexplained reasons why they could not go here or there, why she was at school in

Andalucia, why they lived in Nice and not in England. Why they never went to Great Britain. There were newspapers her mother and father discouraged her from reading. Some of these forbidden papers and periodicals she had none the less perused but had discovered nothing in them of any relevance to her or her life or family.

Nevertheless it was there all the time, in the background, like Banquo's ghost, invisible to everyone yet palpable. An oppressive presence that no one could see but that she felt ever present.

And it was not something nice, this censorship that caused her to examine her sentences before she spoke. Careful what she said.

Her father had a terrible temper. It was wise not to irritate him. He could lose it when people talked of England—like when she suggested they go there for a visit. Why not? She'd never been to her native land. But Victor Sandar had exploded when she had, in all innocence, put the request to him. Or when Maria da Costa asked her to stay with them in their house in Hampstead and Alice's father had, as Alice put it 'lost it completely'. Maria's father was Embassy but her parents wanted her to be educated back home in Spain, so they sent her to the convent. Alice had become friendly with her, insofar as she got close to anyone at all. But Victor Sandar had absolutely forbidden her to entertain the idea of going to London and Alice never dared mention her wish or Maria da Costa again.

She could tell when he was about to lose his temper. She had grown to recognise the signs. A white line would appear around his mouth, his skin would become redly suffused beneath his tan and his eyes would glaze over. Like he'd left his body and someone or something else had invaded his soul. It was terrifying and Alice always found it politic to slip away when it happened. She'd find an excuse—work to do, an appointment to keep—and run fast.

It never lasted long, this fury, and then her father would revert to his usual benign self, lavishing her with love, presents, flattery.

Alice knew too that her mother could provoke that terrible anger quite easily. She decided that families were like that. To her ears, quite innocuous Spanish conversation seemed heated and furious, with gestures and red faces, and she assumed that this was the same kind of conversation that she heard at home, usually after she'd gone to bed.

But most of the time there was peace and Daddy loved his little girl, and Alice was glad to be home. She brushed her hair, cleaned her teeth and ran down the curved staircase and out into the sun for breakfast, ready for Life to happen.

# CHAPTER TWO

The narrow street shimmered with gaudy lights; lurid red, electric blue, violent green, doing a neon dance in the protracted twilight. The street throbbed with the undertow of the drumbeat from the discos and the tiny boutiques on either side. Bustling and crowded, at ten o'clock at night the surging crowds were mainly young, nubile, trawling for adventure, looking for 'the one', boy or girl, whose eyes would light up on contact, instantly spelling romance. It was a forlorn hope, for the eyes were mainly lit by lust, not love.

The older people were dining in their hotels on gigot of lamb, or steak Diane, or glazed this or that and desserts that were works of art. Others were sitting around candlelit tables waited on by white-jacketed servants in their villas high in the hills. The less fortunate came from caravan sites outside the towns—Monte Carlo, Nice, Juan les Pins—and they barbecued on the beach, red as the neon lights after a day toasting themselves in the sun, getting value for money out of the holiday by sunbathing to excess. Now they grilled hamburgers, swilling beer, the men's naked bellies proudly protruding from the drooping band of their shorts.

The narrow street was in the heart of Juan

les Pins where the young gathered and the music was loudest and the atmosphere was charged with adrenalin.

*Vesuvio,* the pizza place and *the* popular rendezvous, was choc-a-block. It was open to the sky, waiters rushing to and fro and the crowd on the pavement dodging the tables as they passed. It was packed with the young, stuffing their faces with different concoctions of delectable pizzas made to order, the best in Juan. Behind the tables on a vast griddle the cooks steamed as they rushed to meet the demand. They chopped red, gold and green peppers, mushrooms, pepperoni and onions red and white, efficiently slinging them on the griddle and removing the browned pastry from the wood-burning ovens to serve the delicious pizzas to the waiting customers.

The girls wore cut-off jeans or khaki shorts and sawn-off tops revealing tanned and taut midriffs, often with a little gold or silver ring piercing the navel. Their hair was newly shampooed and their faces innocent of make-up. 'That tacky gunge' they called it; they did not need it and had the confidence their mothers lacked to do without it.

The young men were dressed in similar fashion though they wore cool cotton shirts or polo tee shirts with the Lacoste, Nike, Calvin Klein or Ralph Lauren logos discreetly woven on pocket-flap, breast or sleeve.

Jonathan Crawley was twenty-four. He wore

9

chinos, a white short-sleeved sea-island cotton shirt and white deck shoes. He was the oldest of the bunch, his teeth extra-white in his sun and wind scorched face, his eyes extra blue. He was the focal point of the conversation, the one to whom the others deferred, maybe because of his age, or maybe because his parents had a large villa on the Cap and were complacent about allowing their son's friends to wander in and out at will. 'Like we hadn't grown,' Jonathan confided.

'Suits me!' Amber remarked. She was often discovered in the Crawley villa curled up in a hammock or dozing on a sun-bed.

'We going to Fat Sam's?' a freckle-faced girl called Charlie asked, licking her fingers one by one. Her red curls were partly held up by a barrette on the top of her head. The barrette had plastic Mickey Mouse discs hanging out of it and she often shook her head, eyes turned upwards, and made them click together like castanets. The rest of her hair curled around her forehead, her neck, and her little pink ears in glossy tendrils.

'Nothin' doin' there.' Jonathan made a face. 'It's a dumb place. Uncool.'

Charlie looked chastened. 'I thought—' She was going to justify her suggestion when the boy beside her, Alastair Darwin, nudged her, throwing a warning glance at her.

'I vote we just hang out here. Maybe.' Alastair sounded doubtful. He nodded to the crowded concourse where gorgeous girls of every nationality paraded—strutting their stuff like sluts, Jonathan had said. The café-bar across the road, *Le Cristal,* was packed. People talked, drank wine or beer, smoked and kissed in the mellow amber light and the fading dusk. The hum of conversation sounded like the roar of the sea.

But they were all in pairs and seemed absorbed in each other.

'Oh shit!' Vinny Maltby cried, shaking his head. 'No joy there. None.'

'I want to find me a babe,' Alastair muttered to Vinny. 'I do, I do. I'm hot tonight.'

'I heard that,' Charlie said.

'So what? We're not joined at the hip.' Alastair sounded peevish. He looked at Jonathan. 'So where? Know so much, where?'

'*Pointe de Diable,*' Jonathan replied promptly. '*The* place. Trust me.'

He knocked back the last of his lager and raised his hand for the waiter.

'*L'addition, s'il vous plait,*' he cried in terrible French.

'My turn,' Alastair muttered half-heartedly and Vinny echoed, 'I'll do it.'

'No,' Jonathan said decisively. 'You always do it, Vinny. Let Alastair.' Then, turning towards the other, 'Alastair, you're such a tight-fisted bastard. Get the bloody bill.'

Amber, a quiet, pale, urchin-like girl, always watching, was picking her nails and pushing them backwards. Her brother drew his breath in through his teeth.

'Don't *do* that Amber,' he hissed.

She paid no attention.

'No use talking,' Jonathan said. 'She won't hear you. She's—'

'What, Jonathan?' Roger leapt to his feet, eager to defend his sister.

'Oh, can it!' Alastair cried irritably.

At that moment something caught Jonathan's eye. He frowned, gazed into the concourse and whispered, 'I don't believe it!' Then he jumped up and leaned over the railing separating the café from the street, yelling, 'Rudi! Rudolph Wolfe! Good God, how extraordinary!'

A young man passing by stopped, the crowd surging past him, parting where he stood against the tide. He looked vaguely around him, wondering where the voice calling his name had come from. He was dark-haired and slim with sleepy eyes, half-closed.

'Who is he?' Charlie asked, perking up, sucking her Diet Coke noisily, her eyes sparkling. 'Wow! He's fit!'

He was indeed good-looking, almost pretty, but his skin was unfashionably pale for this part of the world and his eyes, when looked into closely, seemed to hold ancient sorrows.

'I don't know who he is.' Alastair glanced sourly at Charlie, annoyed. It was one thing for him to go 'chasing skirt', quite another for his

12

open-relationship girlfriend to do ditto. 'He's obviously never heard of fake tan,' he said sourly.

'As you have, Alastair,' Charlie retorted.

'How'd you know?' Alastair, stung, enquired.

'Your hands idiot, your hands are white except the palms. Stained! Sure giveaway,' she giggled.

'He's pale as a white dove,' Amber Crosbie cooed, staring at the newcomer. 'Hair as black as a raven's wing, and eyes as blue as the—'

'What are you on about?' Vinny asked crossly. Anything even vaguely smacking of culture drove him wild. Jonathan said he had an inferiority complex and was jealous because they went to uni and he didn't. He'd dropped out of school—though his mother and father still hadn't sussed this fact. Vinny's mother and father had won twelve million sterling on the lottery and life had never been the same since. They were cruising the coast of Turkey in a luxurious Turkish boat catching up on what they'd missed, they said, and he scarcely saw them. They gave him a huge allowance and the group tolerated him because of the ready money. He was aware that he was not really 'their sort'.

'I'll never have to sweat and toil,' he was fond of saying. 'So what's with the education bit? What's the point of swotting over a lot of dumb stuff that happened yesterday, a decade, a million years ago, huh? Waste of valuable time, if you ask me.'

A huge grin had split the stranger's face.

'Jonathan!' he cried, waving.

Jonathan beckoned him over and he made his way to the table, ambling through the crowds like a hot knife through butter. He reached Jonathan's table, greeting him enthusiastically, and they both stood there slapping shoulders and shaking hands and punching each others chests while Amber watched covertly and Charlie gazed, frankly admiring the newcomer.

Introductions were made, Jonathan enquiring about Rudi's presence here in the South of France, his health, his career and his love life, while at the same time raving about his friend over his shoulder to the others at the table. He kept insisting on how amazed and delighted he was at their unexpected meeting here.

'Jeez, Rudi, it's good to see you. You escaped Bosnia unscathed?'

Alastair and Vinny eyed the newcomer with guarded suspicion, not at all sure they relished the competition. 'Amber Crosbie, that's Roger, her brother in the background. Alastair Darwin and Charlie Fontaine, Vinny Maltby.' Then he turned to them. 'This guy's the best,' he told them.

'He's certainly dishy,' Charlie giggled and the others laughed.

'Oh, Rudi, it's good to see you,' Jonathan insisted. 'Come on. Sit, sit, sit.'

'But you're just leaving.' His accent, Amber decided, was North American. Soft. New England or Canadian, she hazarded a guess.

'Well,' Jonathan hesitated, 'we can stay here awhile.'

'We were going to the *Pointe de Diable,*' Alastair informed the newcomer sourly, and Rudi looked across at him.

There was something disconcerting about the speculative gaze, as if he could see into your head. His eyes were clear, no hidden agenda behind the amused glance. It was a detached assessment and, Alastair feared, summed him up accurately. He was, as they were, in his early twenties, yet he seemed older somehow.

'What are you doing here, old buddy?' Jonathan was asking, sitting again as the waiter came with the bill. Vinny grabbed it and Alastair let him.

'Working,' Rudi said.

'Good grief! No one works here. What a waste!' Alastair protested, laughing a little derisively.

'Lots of people do.' Jonathan sounded as if he were somehow defending his friend's admission. 'Who do you think cooked and served your pizza tonight? Anyhow, *you* do Alastair, so don't get so high and mighty.'

'Tennis coach! Come on! That's not work,'

Alastair blustered a little. He was acutely aware that of the group, he was the only one having to earn his keep.

'Let's go somewhere and have a drink.' Jonathan stood once more. 'Look you guys, you go on to the disco.' He put his hand on Rudi's shoulder. 'We'll have a quick one over there,' he nodded to the café-bar across the street.

'Oh no you don't.' Charlie leapt up and was beside Rudi in a flash. Taking him by the arm she steered him firmly away from the others, propelling him down the Boulevard Baudoin.

They were quick to catch up. Jonathan yelled, 'Just a minute . . . hey!' and ran after them. Vinny threw down some francs. Amber grabbed her cardigan from the back of the chair, Alastair vaulted over a chain-link fence behind him that separated *Vesuvio* from the place next door and they all rushed after the couple who were hurrying away.

'Wait for us!'

Jonathan was furious. Rudi Wolfe had been kidnapped by Charlie and it looked as if *she* was suddenly in charge. He did not want to share his friend with this bunch. Rudi had a habit of attracting people to him and Jonathan felt threatened. He was, after all, leader of the pack. Here at least.

Jonathan's family had been coming to the South of France all of his life. They had a villa on Cap d'Antibes; he knew everyone and

16

everyone knew the Crawleys.

At home, at school then university he had been one of the gang, but here each summer it was different. He was top dog, the guy who knew his way around, knew the 'in' places, knew the right people, knew the fashion, the styles, where to go, what to do. What was cool and what was not.

Rudi Wolfe, it suddenly seemed to Jonathan, was threatening that supremacy. He stared after his friend, out of sorts. Angry.

He should have known better. Whenever he saw Rudi this big wave of emotion engulfed him and he always remembered too late that Rudi, though he did not mean to, stole the limelight, cramped his style. There was something about him, mysterious, remote that drew people to him. He gave the impression of self-containment that was daunting, a confidence that was unconscious, worn easily, needing no one, depending on no other, sophisticated yet also humble in the true sense of the word and unselfish.

To Jonathan's annoyance Charlie had purloined him and the others followed his lead and left him trailing behind. Charlie hung on Rudi's every word, clung to his arm possessively as she trotted along beside him, trying to measure her pace to his faster stride as he hurried up the street pushing against the tide. Alastair dallied a moment, then as Jonathan reached him he fell into step with

17

him and began quizzing him about the newcomer.

'Seems a bit nerdy to me,' he shouted in Jonathan's ear. 'Bit naff!'

'In your dreams!' Jonathan sneered, wishing he could agree. 'Force to be reckoned with,' he added, glancing sourly at his friend ahead of him.

The disco, when they reached it, was as crowded as the street. They converged at the bar, shouting at each other over the noise. The place was bouncing, throbbing, even the stone walls seemed to pulsate and the floor undulate with the heavy beat, the roar of the music and the crush of writhing, leaping, gyrating bodies pounding the earth with primitive energy. Arms were waving high above sweating faces as the dancers poured Evian water from plastic containers down their throats, gulping greedily as they rapidly dehydrated. Some drenched themselves with water as they danced. They were baptising themselves.

The noise was ear-splitting—a nice buzz, Vinny remarked contentedly. Jonathan could not hear what Rudi mouthed at him as Charlie pulled him onto the dance floor. It looked, as he tried to lip-read, suspiciously like 'Help!' He shrugged helplessly as Rudi was swallowed up into the gyrating multitude.

The place was large as an aeroplane hangar, most of it underground. Across the ceiling great tubes or pipes of steel ran in parallel lines. Jonathan never knew whether they were the actual plumbing that connected the lavatories and wash basins, the bars and the beer sinks or just there for decoration. It gave the disco a hellish ambience that suited its name and was compounded by the enormous devil masks, realistic and satanic, that decorated the walls. They were mock-Gothic in style with gaping obscene mouths, enormous angry red eyes and snakes and spiders writhing out of monstrous heads. The lights, swivelling around, caught these gargoyles in their beams every so often and highlighted them to satisfactory horror-inducing effect.

Charlie flirted outrageously with Rudi but very soon after they had begun to jig about on the dancefloor Rudi gave her a twirl and when she turned around he was gone. Charlie looked around her. She stopped waving her arms and moving her body and searched the crowd for him but he'd disappeared. She raked the mob with narrowed eyes trying to peer through the smoke of cigarettes and the steam from evaporating sweat but he was nowhere to be seen. She moved, dancing slowly over towards the party who were now sitting around a table on the balcony just under the tubular pipes.

'He's gone!' she declared when she reached them, raising her shoulders helplessly.

'What've you done with him?' Jonathan

demanded irritably. He'd decided that even though he'd resented Rudi's charisma he wanted him around awhile.

'Nothing. Honest. We were dancing and—'

'You made a move on him! I'll kill you!'

'No. Honest.'

'You cracked on to him. God, you can't be trusted with anything that moves, can you Charlie?'

'I told you, I *didn't*. I hardly exchanged a word with him. You try it out there. What's the matter with you Jonathan? You lost it?'

'I meet one of my oldest, my best friends and ten minutes with you and he's scarpered! What can I say?'

'What's so important about him?' Charlie screamed, annoyed now.

'We share a history, that's all.'

Amber stood up suddenly. 'I need to reach a launch-pad,' she whispered to her brother. Jonathan watched her indifferently as she hurried towards the ladies.

'This place is dead,' he announced. Alastair glanced around the throbbing mass of humanity and laughed.

'If this is dead,' he said, 'then I'll hie me to a graveyard asap. This man is ballistic!' He exchanged glances with a babe in a bikini top and a sarong that looked as if it might drift as the evening progressed.

'What would you know?' Jonathan muttered morosely.

20

'Well, if it's so bad why don't we go to your place?' Vinny suggested. He was always afraid that he might sound uncool which was why he did not agree with Alastair.

Jonathan instantly decided it was a good idea. At his place he was in charge and if they found Rudi, being at the villa, *Beau Rivage*, put him in the driver's seat, no question.

'Okay,' he said. 'Let's go.'

'I want to finish my drink,' Alastair stated reluctantly. The bikini top was working her way towards him across the dance floor.

'Where's Amber gone?' Vinny asked.

'Probably wants a hit,' Roger said almost indifferently.

Alastair looked shocked. 'Not here! Jeez! Tell her to be careful.'

'No. A light hit. Nothing heavy. Know what I mean?'

Charlie was pulling at Jonathan's arm. 'Come on! Let's go! I agree with Jonathan. This place is lame.' And she dragged him after her out of the place. They climbed up into the hot still night and saw Rudi leaning against the stone wall across the street talking to Amber.

'Scabby!' Charlie muttered. 'That's really scabby of Amber.'

'Don't be a pillock, Charlie,' Roger cried. 'My sister is out of it by now. She's no competition.'

'Hey you two, we're going to my place,' Jonathan called. 'C'mon.'

21

Rudi shook his head. 'No. I better get back.'

'Where are you staying?' Jonathan asked.

They stood about waiting uncertainly. The night—every night for them—held the promise of adventure, adventure that never seemed to materialise. Nevertheless each evening revived their hopes. They were terrified that they might miss some opportunity, that there was a party, a happening that they'd somehow not heard of and that they were missing. They hovered, impatient to get going, reluctant to leave. Who knew, the event of the decade might just, could just happen here when they'd gone. It would never do to be in the wrong place at the wrong time.

Rudi was pointing to a *pension,* a tall pretty house down one of the side streets.

'God, it must be hot in there. Bet they haven't got air-conditioning.'

'Sure is,' Rudi admitted regretfully.

'Oh, come on with us to the Cap. It's cool and sweet up there,' Jonathan coaxed. 'You can split early.'

Amber was pulling his sleeve. 'Remember the people you were asking me about? The Sandars? They live next door.'

'What's that about?' Vinny enquired, a puzzled frown on his face.

'I told you. She's out of it,' Roger repeated.

'Besides we haven't caught up,' Jonathan was saying to Rudi. 'I want to know what you've been doing. Word has it that you've been to the war zone. What *are* you doing here? You're sure not coaching tennis.' He laughed.

Rudi gave in with good grace and they piled into Vinny's car, Charlie and Amber jockeying for position on either side of him in the back and Alastair in the front with Vinny. Jonathan, to his annoyance, was left on his own. Charlie waved saucily at him as Vinny pulled out and reversed behind him and Jonathan gripped the wheel, fumed, then led them slowly in his MG through the crowded streets, then up the winding road to his parents' villa on the Boulevard du Cap.

## CHAPTER THREE

'Welcome,' Angelica Crawley smiled at the group as they rounded the corner from the gravel driveway where they'd parked the cars. They came through an old stone archway thick with wisteria onto the terrace.

'God, the wrinklies are at home!' Jonathan cried, aghast, not bothering to conceal his irritation.

Angelica heard her son. 'Come on in then pimplies,' she beckoned, smiling evilly. Alastair and Charlie touched their faces involuntarily.

Jonathan's parents had dinner guests, eight

of them, all seemingly cast in the same mould. Their attention was focused politely on the young people at whom they smiled mechanically. Seated around the candlelit table, the women were elegantly dressed and the men wore white tuxedos. Their faces had the weatherbeaten look of sun-worshippers or yachtspeople. Two white-uniformed servants were serving coffee. The young people, trying to evade this concerted interest in them, hurried past hoping to escape the amused superior scrutiny. They were unaware that the amused superior scrutiny concealed a terrible jealousy of their youth.

'You've eaten?' Angelica asked.

'We were in *Vesuvio*,' Jonathan volunteered.

'Stuffing yourselves with junk!' Angelica made a face. 'Then off, off, off!' She waved a hand dismissing them and turned to her left, continuing her conversation with a famous but ageing film star whose dyed black hair and eyebrows made him look even older than he actually was.

Brompton Crawley had not acknowledged his son's presence. He was deep in conversation, puffing on an illegally imported Havana cigar, his head shrouded in clouds of smoke. He had turned his chair at the top of the table to face a walnut-bronzed man who sat stone still facing the sea. Alastair sniggered and the man suddenly looked up at them, catching Rudi's eye in a glance from the grave.

24

Icy cold, curiously venomous, his eyes nevertheless seemed dead. Alastair glanced at Rudi and his mirth shrivelled up instantly.

'Who's that?' he whispered to Rudi.

'That is Victor Sandar,' Rudi replied.

Alastair hated to admit it but Jonathan's parents and their friends, petrified him. There was something mocking about them. Knowing, jaded, yet sharp; he always felt naked in their presence.

The villa looked out over the bay. Decorated with a necklace of lights circling the coast, above them the sky was encrusted with stars. The Greek-columned house faced the sea, a blue velvet cloak in the distance. On one side a square paved loggia encompassed the dining area, the kitchens behind it in the house, and on the other side a rose-entwined gazebo nestled on the immaculate lawn. The boundary there was marked by cedars and pine trees which tried, not entirely successfully, to cut off the view to the left.

Jonathan's group crossed the open terrace, waving to the chattering diners. They slunk across to the other side eager not to be hailed by one of the guests who perchance knew a father or mother and would try to engage in 'freaky' conversation.

The French windows were open, lights burning in the spacious rooms inside, but they did not look in; they were all familiar with the house. Every now and then there was a sizzling sound as another mosquito hit the dust, irresistibly drawn to the electric-blue zappers. The group meandered to the gazebo and sat clustered on the stone seats or lounging against the moonlit pillars discontentedly grumbling at the lack of action.

'Might as well be one of the wrinklies,' Alastair muttered, thinking regretfully of the hot eyes of the bikini-clad babe in the disco.

'Might as well be dead,' Charlie moaned.

Amber had plucked a branch of ivy and was winding it around Rudi's head. He was still as a statue staring down through the trees. His breathless immobility attracted the attention of the others as they grouped together to try to see what he saw.

'What is it?'

'What's there?'

The villa beside and below *Beau Rivage*, the *Villa Bella Vista*, was further down the hillside, the grounds terraced down to the sea. Following Rudi's gaze they could see through the barrier of the trees the swimming pool below them.

They watched breathlessly, all of them fixed on the sight that had grabbed Rudi's attention.

The swimming pool in the villa was a vivid aquamarine, lit from beneath, rippling gently under the golden moon, bathed in a reflected azure light. It glimmered and glittered in the dark.

A girl had come out from the villa into the

stillness. From the warm amber lights of the house she emerged into the pale moonlight like a wraith. She moved soundlessly, a vision from a fairytale. She was completely naked, a sylph, a nymph, perfect in every clean smooth limb, each muscle firm and toned, a body miraculously beautiful and cared for. Her hair flowed in a golden tumble down her back and she was obviously sure she was alone, completely unconscious of their attention, enveloped in a mysterious separateness as if she were not of this world.

Her appearence had struck the little group in the gazebo dumb. The harsh chorus of the cicadas sawed the air all around them and from a distance the sound of Jonathan's parents' sharp laughter and the buzz of their conversation from afar blended with the hum of the traffic above them on the boulevard.

There was something remote about the girl, utterly unselfconscious as she went to the diving board and, arching her back, stretching her arms above her head, every ligament and muscle taut, she raised one knee then leapt, ballerina-like, her movement full of power and grace. Like a golden arrow, she sliced into the still aquamarine water of the pool.

She hardly made a sound, simply a sharp crack as the diving board jack-knifed and a little whisper of the water as her body cleft the pool and the breathless moment was over.

For some reason the group remained silent.

They moved, shifted their attention but they did not, as they would normally, cat-call, whoop or in some way herald their presence and try to embarrass the girl.

Their concentration splintered as one of the servants approached from the opposite side of the villa with a tray of drinks. Chilled champagne and peach juice made from the luscious white peaches of Provence.

'Madame say, you not like, you have beer, Coca-Cola, whatever you want,' the Filipino man said loudly, his eyes blinking. Exiled, desperate to make money and rescue his family from abject poverty, he was subservient and eager to please.

They took the tulip glasses, oblivious of him. He could have been a robot for all the acknowledgement they gave him. They drank and only Rudi remained watching the girl.

She could not hear them for she was underwater. When she surfaced she turned her face upwards towards their voices and Rudi's heart sped on a crash course with his ribs. The hectic tattoo it beat was almost painful as he stared at the perfect oval, the meltingly soft brown eyes, startled, vulnerable, spotlit by the pool lights.

She stared into the thick shadowed foliage dappled by the ground lights, as if she sensed a presence there, lurking, watching, though he knew she could not possibly see him. He felt momentarily ashamed and tried to turn away and join the others but it was as if he were hypnotised and could not deflect his gaze. She flipped her legs, scissoring them as she swam to the side of the pool where she picked up a white towel from a huge basket and wrapped it carefully, meticulously around herself, conscious now that she might be observed.

Jonathan glanced over his shoulder as Rudi left the gazebo. 'Come on,' he called. Rudi joined Jonathan on the terrace with the others. They were discussing where they should go, what they could do to relieve their boredom.

'Who is she?' Rudi asked his friend.

'Alice Sandar,' he replied, shaking his head, knowing instantly who Rudi meant. 'Bad news. Bad, *bad* news. She's the daughter of the infamous Victor Sandar.' He jerked his head back towards his parents' dinner table. 'The chap talking to my father.'

'Oh hell!' Rudi grimaced.

Jonathan glanced at his friend. Rudi's usually enigmatic expression was now one of irritation.

'You know him?' Jonathan asked.

'I know *of* him,' Rudi replied.

'I'm not surprised,' Jonathan remarked. He sipped his drink. 'You okay? You look a bit . . .' He shook his head and left the sentence hanging.

'I don't think I've ever seen anyone so beautiful in my whole life,' Rudi said softly and Jonathan snorted. He was very like his mother at that moment.

'Oh, better steer clear of that one, mate,' he said. 'That's forbidden fruit, and I mean *verboten*! Unless you're prepared to be rubbed out! Blown away,' he explained, raising two fingers and mock shooting himself with them through his temple. 'We don't even look,' he added. 'She's, like, *lethal*.'

Rudi turned his head and Jonathan could see his eyes glittering like bright lights in the dusk.

'What do you mean?' Rudi asked breathlessly. Even as he asked, he could see that flippant though his tone, Jonathan was obviously nervous.

'Old Victor,' Jonathan told his friend, 'dotes on his daughter. He is—how shall I put it— possessive to say the least. Very possessive. And you know his reputation.'

Rudi shrugged. 'Well, I've heard stories.'

'He's a villain, Rudi.' Jonathan was whispering, as if he was afraid of being overheard. 'He's ruthless. No morals. No boundaries. He doesn't like you, you offend him, you're dead.'

'No kidding!'

Jonathan drew back, staring at his friend skeptically. 'You having me on? You musta . . . *Everyone* knows about Victor Sandar. Like John Gotti . . .'

'He's Mafia.'

'Well, Sandar isn't.' Jonathan shook his

head impatiently. 'He's English.'

'Oh, well then. How'd you expect me—'

'But you're a journalist.'

'British gangsters, I don't know *that* much about them. 'Course, I've *heard* things.'

'Well, I would have thought . . .' Jonathan shrugged and the two friends strolled back towards the gazebo.

It was deeply shadowed and they could hardly see each other in the dark. They drank for a moment in silence, then Jonathan said, 'You haven't told me what you're doing here, Rudi. You said you were working.'

'Yeah,' Rudi hesitated. 'The jazz festival in Juan. I'm doing a piece for *Newsdesk* on all the old guys, you know.'

'I didn't think that was your field?'

'Oh yes. Love it. It's about the emergence of jazz in France. *Le Jazz Hot*, you know. Bix Beiderbecke. Charlie Parker.'

Jonathan knew that for some reason Rudi was lying, or at least not telling the full truth. He decided to leave the subject.

'Makes a change from Bosnia,' Rudi said.

'Jeez, man! You really went there, then?'

Rudi nodded but kept silent and Jonathan knew he had no intention of discussing it any further. He was sipping his drink, his long body relaxed, his face shuttered. Every now and then he glanced at the next-door pool through the curtain of leaves and branches, the verdant foliage.

'Come on,' Charlie called from the terrace. 'We're going to have a game of pool.'

Rudi looked at Jonathan who said, 'We got a table. In the games room. Beside the tennis courts.' The tennis courts were on the other side of the villa, near the entrance. Rudi smiled at Jonathan and shook his head.

'Funny you've never been here before, all the years I've known you.'

'Yeah.'

'Coming?'

'Leave me here a moment. I'll come down in a while.'

'Keep off that though,' Jonathan jerked his head in the direction of the villa next door. 'Not worth it,' he told his friend and he followed the others back across the terrace.

'Wanna bet?' Rudi muttered softly and swallowed the last of the champagne.

## CHAPTER FOUR

The fences around the property were electrified and there were video cameras at strategic points in the grounds and on the building, moving around in slow motion. There were two rottweilers with evil faces looking, Rudi thought, not unlike the satanic paintings in the *Pointe du Diable*. He opted for the cedar. It was old and gnarled but strong and he scaled its branches with agility, climbing like a monkey until he was high above both villas and he could look down on them from his lofty position. He searched for a suitably strong bough, tested it, found it bore his weight, then shifting himself into position he sat on it, legs dangling over. It gave with him a little like a trampoline and for a moment he thought it must snap. But it held and he settled himself as comfortably as he could, looking down at where Alice lay on the cream-coloured lounger, the white towel cuddled closely around her, her cheek on her hand.

She looked asleep, her long lashes resting on sun-tinted cheeks, her other hand curled beside her face like a baby's.

'Hi.' He said it softly so as not to startle her. Her eyelids flew open and with a quick fierce intake of breath she sat up. Her eyes were alarmed.

'Who's there?' It was a whisper and she scanned the bushes, the shadowy corners of the garden, looking down the terraces to where the fountain gushed. The ground lights were all on and they filtered through the leaves and caught the wavering reflection of the pool and dappled the garden in shimmering rays. It seemed as if the whole garden was underwater and she was a sea nymph lying in translucent radiance.

Her eyes were raking the gliding shadows but she could not locate him.

'Up here,' he said in an even tone, his voice firm and unafraid, yet still soft and calm not to alarm her.

She looked up and saw him and her eyes widened.

Then she grinned. 'You look like a heavenly apparition,' she laughed but glanced nervously back over her shoulder to the house. Then she added, 'Santa Maria de Compostella. Saint Theresa. Bernadette.'

'They're all female!'

'Oh Lord!'

'No! No, I'm certainly not him.' He laughed with her, his heart stabbed by a passionate yearning that cut his laugh short and made him gasp in pain.

Her face became serious. She frowned and he thought her more beautiful than the saints she had mentioned.

'What are you doing there?' she asked a little testily.

'Looking at you,' he answered.

She pulled the towel closer around her body.

'That's not fair.'

'You are!'

'It's against the law.'

'I know. I could go to prison. But it would be worth it!'

'You're a Peeping Tom!' She was laughing again in spite of herself.

'Peeping Toms don't try to get acquainted.

34

They're secretive and nasty. I'm not nasty.'

Again she glanced nervously into the villa behind her, then shrugged and said with mock severity, 'Well, I wouldn't know about that now, would I? I'm not in the habit of getting chummy with Peeping Toms.'

As she spoke a stout black-clad matron emerged from the house. The girl looked and Rudi kept very still.

'Alice? Alice? You talkin' to someone?'

Rudi put his finger to his lips. 'Please,' he begged.

'No, Nana. Whatever gave you that idea?'

The woman advanced across the terrace and stood behind the lounger.

'Ugh! It's gettin' damp. You best come in now,' she told the girl. 'At once. You hear me. You'll catch your death of cold if you stay out here.'

'I'll come in a moment, Nana,' the girl said but the woman persisted. 'No. You come in right now. What would your Daddy say?'

She was not to be appeased and the girl rose obediently and, holding the white towel around her, allowed herself to be hustled inside without a backward glance.

The woman went on gently scolding as they left.

'Your Mamma, she's drinking coffee in the rose arbour out front. You want to join her?' And the sliding window was closed behind them, cutting off all sound.

Rudi sighed. All the light seemed to have followed the girl indoors and it was suddenly dark, bleak and uncomfortable, perched in the tree, awkwardly hanging onto the branch. But he stayed there, unwilling to break the spell, cut the moment short and climb down. He did not want to end the enchantment and return to ordinary things. The thought of a pool game filled him with dread and he sat there, swinging his legs like a recalcitrant schoolboy.

How long he sat there he did not know, but his legs were getting pins and needles when a fierce shaft of bright light suddenly pierced the darkness around him and he blinked. The shutters were flung open and Alice stood there in the second-floor window on the little balcony in a virginal white lawn nightgown that completely covered her body, neck to toe. He caught his breath at her beauty. His heart seemed to fly right out of his body at the sight of her.

'Hello again,' he whispered nervously. Nothing in his past experience with girls had prepared him for this deprivation of all his defences, this utter enslavement. He was stripped of confidence, calm and control all in a second, left staring open-mouthed at her like a teenager on his first date.

'Who are you?' she asked, her voice soft as a kitten's purr.

'I'm Rudi,' he replied and in contrast his voice sounded harsh.

'Rudi who?'

'Wolfe.'

'Like Little Red Riding Hood,' she smiled.

'Oh no!' His protest was sincere, heartfelt and she laughed. 'I'm not like that,' he cried.

'I didn't really think you were.'

'Who you talkin' to?' It was the woman again. He recognised the voice. 'You goin' crazy? Close them shutters y'hear? Lettin' in the mosquitoes!' The voice came from behind the girl from what was obviously Alice's bedroom.

'All right, Nana. In a moment,' Alice called back.

'I said who you talkin' to?'

'The stars, Nana. The stars,' Alice cried back and this time it was she who put her finger to her lips and shook her head.

There was the sound of a door closing in the room, then the girl leaned forward, her nightdress a white cloud about her, her hair flowing over her shoulders like spun gold.

'I've got to go in,' she said.

'Why did you come out?' he asked. She hesitated, lowered her chin, then looked up at him. 'I wanted . . . I wanted to see if you were still there,' she whispered. 'To see if I had been dreaming.'

'You'd dream of me?' he asked. She did not answer but her eyes were full of a kind of ardent hopefulness.

A big moonlike face was suddenly thrust out

37

of the window cutting Alice from his sight. He leaned back, lost his balance and fell onto the grass below him.

'What's that?' he heard the woman ask. 'I heard somethin'. I know I did.'

'It was the dogs, Nana,' the enchantress replied in a smooth voice. 'There's nothing there at all.'

'Well, you come in now.'

'Yes, yes, Nana.' Then he heard Alice but could not see her. 'You all right?' She sounded anxious.

'Yes,' he called up reassuringly. Then added, 'Do you care?'

The woman's voice had not stopped its hectoring and now became audible again, near the balcony. 'I don't know what your father would say, you out in the damp night air talkin' to the stars! I never heard such nonsense.' A click-clicking of her tongue and the clash of shutters folding up and then darkness. Nana had gathered her charge in for the night.

## CHAPTER FIVE

Rudi picked himself up. Bemused, he brushed himself down. He felt intoxicated, in a turmoil, not at all in charge of himself as he usually was. He felt high as a kite, curiously tearful and raw with emotion. In short he felt he was in shock.

Jonathan was calling him. He could hear the click-click of balls as he crossed the terrace, past the front of the house. He could see the diners who were, or seemed to be in exactly the same position as when the group had passed them by. How long ago? It seemed a lifetime to Rudi. He glanced covertly at the walnut-faced man, Victor Sandar, *her* father. The divinity's father! He was a silhouette at this distance sitting motionless beside his host. There was something curiously menacing about him, though Rudi wondered if it was merely his overwrought imagination.

'Young man! Young man! Wheel me to the table, there's a dear.'

He nearly fell over the wheelchair which suddenly erupted through the French windows in front of him.

He looked down. There was a tiny birdlike woman propelling herself less than smoothly along in the chair. She was heavily made up, her sparse eyelashes clotted with mascara, her lips a lurid purple and a round patch of cerise on each cheek. She wore a Juliet cap on thinning indeterminate hair but in spite of this, Rudi decided, she was very beautiful. Her enormous violet eyes were like great depthless orbs that fairly sparkled with intelligence. The stained mouth had an incurably humorous twist. The woman tried to look severe and forbidding but without much success. Her cheekbones were exquisitely formed and her nose-tip tilted, so that her whole bearing was regal but somehow pert.

'Of course,' he said, trying to collect himself, return to some semblence of sanity. He smiled at her. 'Where would you like to go?'

'Like? *Like?* To the gaming tables or the *Negresco* for a drink,' she told him. 'But alas that's not on the cards, is it?' She sighed regretfully, cocking her head, peering at him quizzically, a devil sparking her eyes.

'What about back to the table? That be all right?' he asked. He felt like adding, 'Your Majesty', but refrained.

'*Mon Dieu*, do I have to?' she cried despairingly. 'They are the most boring people I've ever had the misfortune to meet.' She shook her head. 'Except for that terrible man, Victor Sandar, who always gives me the shivers, which,' she rolled her eyes, 'is at least *something*. The others leave me . . . not exactly cold, worse, sort of lukewarm. Right-wing idiots!'

'Oh dear!' His interest had been instantly aroused at the name Sandar. 'Which one is he? Victor Sandar I mean,' he asked, just to verify.

'There! Look,' she indicated the table where the walnut-faced man was sitting, listening with hooded eyes to his host who was still turned to him, talking. 'As if you could mistake him. He has a menace about him. It emanates from him.' She was whispering now, her voice

40

holding a kind of awe. Then she shivered with mock horror. 'He might be planning another murder. Our host's, perhaps! Brompton would strain anyone's patience. Always waffling on! Never waiting for a reply! Not at all amusing.'

'You know Victor Sandar well?' Rudi asked. She suddenly looked furtive and lowered her eyes.

'Why do you ask that?'

'Well, you sound—'

'We were lovers,' she said. 'Once, long ago.'

Her face had collapsed into an ancient sadness.

'I'm sorry,' he said, 'I didn't mean to pry.'

'No, no. You're not. It was long ago and far away, and,' she added, 'I think he has forgotten. Or he pretends he has. Like many men he is quite sure old age will never come to *him*. To everyone else, yes. But not to him. And old lovers tend to remind one that we are not as young as we think we are, or we would like to think we are.'

He was standing behind the wheelchair, listening, holding the handles and on a sudden impulse he bent down and asked, 'Do you really want to go to the casino or the *Negresco*?'

She turned her head and looked at him, eyes wide and full of mischief. She nodded eagerly, like a child.

'Sure I do,' she cried emphatically. She looked suddenly young and he marvelled at

41

how beautiful she must have been long ago.

'Then allow me to escort you,' he said. 'Perhaps not to Monte Carlo, but for a drink, a nightcap at the *Negresco*?'

She gave an excited squeal. 'Oh, would you? Oh my goodness, this is exciting. It is a very, very long time since a beautiful young man escorted me anywhere. Are you sure?' She peered at him, then waved her hand as if to dismiss an unpleasant thought. 'No, I won't press my luck. You might change your mind. I'm not going to speculate whether you are sincere. Yes, yes, yes. Let's go. You and me. But don't let's tell the others or they'll all want to come and I've had quite enough of that lot for one evening.' Then she clapped her hand to her mouth. 'Oh, I do hope your mother or father are not there?'

He shook his head. There were so many questions he wanted to ask her, so much he wanted to know.

'We haven't been introduced,' she said, twisting her head to see him. 'I am the Comtesse de Sevigné, better known as Nola Reine.'

He remembered her then, recalled her face. The film star who'd shone with a brilliant luminous light in the forties and early fifties, then abruptly retired from the screen while still at her zenith. They said she'd never made a bad movie, that all her films were classics. She'd married; first a hunk called Brent

42

Charles. She'd co-starred with him in five classic sophisticated comedies. He'd been a perfect foil for her as he was not merely a gorgeous specimen of manhood but a gifted comedian and could match her cool beauty and perfect comedy timing. Then, Rudi vaguely remembered reading that there was some scandal, something unsavoury though he could not recall what and she'd left Hollywood under a cloud, dropped out of sight. She'd briefly hit the gossip columns in Europe, when she'd met and married a Comte something or another, obviously this de Sevigné. She'd faded from the American tabloids, swallowed up in the less publicised European social scene.

It was all Rudi could remember, though he'd written about her indirectly. He'd recently done a profile of Brent Charles when, amid a lot of Hollywood brouhaha and pizazz the star reached his seventieth birthday. *Fifty Wonderful Years in Movies,* Rudi's piece for his magazine had been called.

Rudi had, of course, researched the star's marriages for the article. He'd interviewed Mr Charles but the famous face became firmly shuttered at the mention of his first wife, Nola Reine, and Rudi had felt it politic not to probe. All he could remember about the little lady in the wheelchair he was pushing towards the table was that Nola had been the number one box office draw in her day. He was very hazy about what exactly the scandal was that drove her out of Hollywood.

'I'm Rudolph Wolfe,' he told her as he began to roll the chair across the terrace.

'How de do!' she laughed coyly, batting her heavily mascared eyelashes at him.

'Nola darling!' Angelica Crawley, catching sight of them, rose from the table and moved towards them as they approached. 'My dear, did you find it?'

Nola turned her head to Rudi behind her and muttered out of the corner of her mouth. 'She's talkin' about the can!' He burst out laughing.

Angelica frowned. 'What's so funny?' she asked, then continued, 'We're wheelchair-friendly here. No awkward steps and lots of handles to grab.' She winked. 'You see, my dear mother is physically challenged,' she confided knowingly. She nodded at Nola who cried in horror, 'I am *not* like your mother.'

Angelica's hand flew to her mouth. 'Oh heavens, I didn't mean . . . I meant *as well*. My mother is physically challenged as you are. Too,' she faltered, obviously terrified she'd made a gaffe.

Nola's face hardened. 'Why do you have to pussyfoot around?' she cried. 'Your mother and I are cripples, for God's sake! Spit it out woman! Spit it out!'

Angelica had turned bright red and was obviously floundering. Rudi, trying to put her out of her misery, said, 'I'm taking the

44

Comtesse home.'

'Are you sure, Nola dear?' Angelica sounded tentative, almost relieved the film star was leaving. Rudi decided that Nola Reine was probably not the ideal guest.

Angelica frowned at Rudi. 'And who are you?' she asked.

'A friend of your son's. Jonathan and I were at college together. Rudolph Wolfe.'

Her face cleared. 'Rudi! Of course. Why didn't you say so? You stayed with us once at Hartley Manor didn't you? Jonathan is always talking about you.'

Rudi doubted that very much. Jonathan had a mind like a grasshopper and out of sight was out of mind with him. Rudi was, however, glad enough at her acceptance of him because he wanted nothing more now than to escape with Nola Reine and talk to her about Victor Sandar.

He got the little Comtesse to her car and lifted her inside with Angelica's blessing. She was light as a feather and he was moved by the feel of her fragile bones beneath his hands as he deposited her in the front seat. All this time the click-clacking of the billiard balls sounded in the background and occasional cheers and yells came from the open doors far right of the loggia. The sound of his friends at play.

\*       \*       \*

Nola Reine had dismissed her chauffeur in a very grand manner and, as the Comtesse's Pontiac—driven by Rudi—purred into the distance, Jonathan Crawley emerged from the billiard room. Rudi waved without turning in the driving seat.

'Where on earth is he off to?' Jonathan called out into the night.

'Who, dear?' Angelica enquired.

'Rudi Wolfe,' her son shouted back over the noise of the retreating engine. 'Has he kidnapped the girl next door? He was certainly smitten with her.'

Jonathan had his back to the diners so he did not see the walnut-faced man—who had appeared to be dozing—raise his head sharply, his eyes narrowing, shooting sparks at Jonathan's remark. He rose briskly, waving at the cigar smoke. He swung away from the table and left, abruptly calling out, 'Night all! Angelica, Brompton, night.' He disappeared towards the back of the villa where a little path a quarter of a mile long led down the incline to the villa next door, the villa where the girl had been.

'A very nice-looking young man he is too,' Angelica was saying. 'Do bring him again, Jonathan.'

'But where is he?' Jonathan yelled.

'*So* considerate!' Angelica enthused. 'He's taken the Comtesse home, dear.'

'Oh Mother! He's *not* a chauffeur,'

Jonathan protested. 'Honestly! I wish you wouldn't press-gang my friends . . .'

'I did not!' she interrupted indignantly, 'It was a *fait accompli*. He came from the house wheeling her.'

'*Wheeling?*' Jonathan exclaimed incredulously. 'He's wheeling who?'

'She's physically challenged dear. Like Grandma. Um, er, crip . . . oh dear!'

'*Mother!* Well, that must have made his night! He must be thrilled to bits, driving some *physically challenged* old biddy home, some old wrinkly!' He started back to where a concerted yell told them that something exciting had happened in the game.

'He could always have said no,' Angelica protested after him.

'No Mother, not Rudi. He's far too polite,' Jonathan told her, tight-lipped. He left her standing there uncertainly as he hurried back to the billiard game muttering, 'Bloody parents! No shit, they're embarrassing! And we never talked! Oh hell.'

## CHAPTER SIX

The lounge in the *Negresco* had the old-world opulence without any of the faded grandeur one sometimes found in Grand Hotels of that ilk. Rudi found a sofa in a quiet corner and settled the two of them over small Napoleon brandies.

The pace here was the opposite of the frenetic activity and bustle in Juan les Pins. Slow and measured as a minuet. Exquisitely dressed bejewelled women in evening frocks and men in bespoke tailored dinner jackets, mainly white and cream, moved in a stately pavane across carpeted and marble floors attended by immaculate waiters, bell-boys and bartenders. The atmosphere was muted, the appointments luxurious, the flower arrangements spectacular. No voices were raised, all was hushed and quiet.

There were hardly any young people there and Rudi felt conspicuous in his Levis, white tee shirt and navy blazer.

'Now young man, what's this all about?' Nola enquired when they were settled. She examined him quizzically. 'Don't think I believe for one moment it's my fatal charm that's prompted you to satisfy an old lady's whim. Those days are, sadly, over. No, I've got something you want, am I right?'

He would have liked to pump her for information undetected, but he ruefully decided she was too smart for that and he'd best be selectively honest with her, otherwise she'd twig and perhaps clam up.

'Yes, Comtesse, you have,' he admitted.

'I thought so.' She nodded, then relaxed. 'Call me Nola,' she said. 'If you'd denied it I'd not have told you a thing—so there. I can be very contrary.' She cocked her head. 'So, what do you want to know? What's so important you'd give up an evening raving it up in a disco with your friends to take an old lady on a secret rendezvous?'

'Okay, Nola. It's about Sandar. I need to know about Victor Sandar.'

She let out her breath slowly. 'Ah!' she said softly. 'Why? Now don't lie to me, Rudi.' She took an ivory holder from her purse, a Gauloise cigarette, and putting it in the holder waited for Rudi to light it. He complied to her unspoken request with a match taken from a book on the table in front of them. Then he leaned forward looking at her intently.

'No. This is the truth Nola. The absolute truth. I fell for you the moment we met. I mean it. You're my kind of dame,' he mugged like Cagney. 'Seriously. And I might well have brought you here for no other reason than your company. But—'

'Ah, a but. You also want to know things?'

He nodded. 'Yeah. I want to know things that you know.'

'Why? Again, the truth please.'

He thought of Alice's radiant face, her wide innocent eyes, her heartstopping smile. And he thought of the other reason. Which to confess to her? Which would be the one most likely to prompt her to confide in him? He juggled them a moment in his head and plumped for the former.

'I'm in love with his daughter,' he stated firmly.

She stared at him, eyes widening. *'Mon Dieu!'* she exclaimed. *'Oh, Mon Dieu.* Poor doomed man.' She took a sip of her brandy, patted his knee and shook her head. 'You have no idea what you are up against,' she murmured.

'Tell me.'

'Have you got time?'

'All the time in the world when it comes to Alice.'

'You'll need it,' she said and, settling back in her chair on the sofa, she instructed him to get comfortable. 'It's a long story,' she said, and began to talk.

## CHAPTER SEVEN

The story began, she told him, in the forties. A young man driving a Duesenberg coupé caught the eye of a lovely neglected actress.

The California sunshine winked on the windscreen of his up-to-the-minute car and the tanned young man leapt over the half-door and out onto the gravel. Hurrying over to the film actress and falling on one knee, he declared his undying love for her. It was extravagant, amusing and romantic and it grabbed her.

Brent was not around at the time. Brent in fact was never around. They'd only been married six months when, she told Rudi, she'd discovered him in bed with her stand-in. 'He had the original at home and here he was screwing the stand-in, for Christ's sake! You ever heard the like? Well Rudi, what I didn't know, but what everyone else in the colony knew was that Brent Charles screwed everything that moved. It was like, he was so insecure, all the adulation he was getting, he didn't quite believe it. He had to prove, *endlessly* prove he was Mister Macho. Numero Uno. Top Gun. Every five minutes. With *anyone.*'

The small, aged elfin face was turned to him in disbelief. 'Priapic they call it. It's an illness. Can you believe it?'

'No. It's difficult.'

'The big baboon! I loved him and for a long time I tried to find excuses for him, believed he'd change. Grow up. But he eventually wore out my patience and my respect.' She glanced at Rudi. 'I'm a proud woman, Rudi. I couldn't take the gossip. The pity in people's eyes. Nola Reine, number one sex symbol, has everything but she can't keep her man. They were laughing at me, ridiculing me. Me and Rock Hudson. Everyone knew Rock was gay, as they call it now, homosexual. They sneered in a superior sort of way and the studios kept the lid on it, terrified it would get out and his fans—mainly women—would go right off him. Money was at the bottom of it, of course. They stood to lose a fortune if it came out that Rock was gay and that Brent was indiscriminate. Poor Nola, her husband a prize stud, but not with her, with every starlet, call girl, anyone would do. They blamed *me*—as if I could help it.

'We had separate bedrooms. Gossip columnists like Louella Parsons and Hedda Hopper knew all about it. Every so often they'd print a warning in their articles, "If a certain bombshell, number one at the box office does not satisfy her man there will be tears eventually", and "Rock, dragging you heels in the marriage market will not help your career!" The studios would rear up and threaten us. There was the morality code. You could be deported! Look what happened to Ingrid Bergman. Banned in the United States Congress from setting foot in the hypocritical USA because she committed adultery. Dear, dear, dear! As if half, no, three-quarters of the politicians weren't doing the same! Only they weren't found out—as they say, the only sin is to be discovered. It was a farce, but then morality in America *is* a farce. There is nothing so distasteful as the sight of the righteous lynch mob in action. Christianity? Hell no. It's Old Testament stuff that Jesus Christ came to modify. Turn the other cheek, he said, forgive, forgive, forgive. Don't cast the first stone. *That's* Christianity.

'Well, there I was on the lawn, the studio's prisoner, under oath never to breathe a word about Brent's infidelities, to deny we were anything but idyllically happy, to play the ideal couple for the benefit of the American public when life was hell in reality for me, when this young man bursts onto my lawn in the middle of one of my cocktail parties and declares his undying love for me. He couldn't have come at a more opportune time.

'I was bruised, Rudi. My spirit was crushed. I felt like a paper cut-out, all façade and nothing behind. I responded to this impetuous chap with amused tolerance, but I was touched. Impressed.' Her eyes were soft with remembering. Her whole face had become fuzzy with tenderness. 'He pursued me relentlessly from that day on. He was always around, but discreetly. He constantly proved his love for me in a thousand little ways and I lapped it up. Each of his loving actions wore down my defences.

'I got a terrible allergy. I was always getting allergies in California. I came up with lumps all over my face and chest. Not a pretty sight. They had to suspend shooting. It was,' she paused, thinking, wrinkling her forehead, then clicking her fingers. '*The Statesman's Daughter*,' she cried. 'That was it. And Brent was opposite me. Well, I looked like a pickled gherkin. Everyone fled. Brent was disgusted. Wouldn't look at me. Not that he ever saw that much of me, just the scenes we acted together. At home he came in the back entrance. Avoided my rooms.' She looked across at Rudi, her eyes brilliant and hard and full of ancient pain. 'And at this time we were "America's Happiest Couple", "America's Perfect Pair". Oh, it truly was a farce!

'Anyhow, my guy in the Duesenberg was faithful. He didn't mind about my face. He came to see me in my sickbed. I got my maid Berthe to let him in. She thought I was crazy. "You like a turkey," she told me and I thought, This will put him off. If he's starstruck, in love with my screen image, the glamour, well then, this will give him a shock. He'll soon cool his heels and flee the sickroom.

'No chance! He was respectful, adoring. There, every day, bringing gifts, flowers, candy, books he thought would amuse me.

'When I was recovering we crept out at night down to a little fish restaurant near the beach. We had supper there. No one paid any attention to us and it became a habit. He made me laugh. It's so sexy, isn't it? Laughing together.' She sighed. 'He was very handsome. But ruthless.' She frowned and her high forehead wrinkled like crumpled tissue paper. 'There was something about him. A quality. You knew he'd get what he wanted. You *knew*. It both frightened and thrilled me. This ruthlessness in him. He gave me the feeling that I could just surrender and I'd be safe, oh so safe and cared for in his hands.' She shrugged, the shoulders sharp and thin beneath the black chiffon of her gown. 'And inevitably I did. Surrender. Ah, it was such a relief, to give up, give in. So seductive. Like an old Valentino movie,' she sighed nostalgically. 'And he was a wonderful lover, strong, tender.'

She glanced again at Rudi. 'He always had plenty of money but I didn't know what he did, how he got it. He never said, and I didn't ask because,' she bit her lip, 'I guess I was afraid of what he'd say. I sussed there was something not quite right, but I guess I didn't want to have to face a moral dilemma. Like if he was married. Like if he was a crook. Hollywood in those days was full of crooks. One didn't ask. I didn't want to break the glorious spell.'

There was a pause. Silence. A tall blonde in a fishtail scarlet satin evening dress swayed in on the arm of an ancient, wizened man, covered in gold jewellery. She was very beautiful, though to Rudi her eyes seemed glazed and lifeless. Like the little angel fish swimming in the tank in the French fishmongers below in the port.

Nola saw him staring and followed his gaze. 'Lauretta Carmentana,' she supplied. 'A bankable star, Rudi. Coked up as usual. Comatose. Feeling no pain. Sometimes it is all we can do, anaesthetise ourselves.'

55

'Did you?' he asked.

She shook her head firmly, the jewelled Juliet cap twinkling under the lights as she moved. 'No. I liked to be in control. And I liked to—' she frowned, searching for the right word, '—*participate* in my life. Even the bad bits. Not miss anything. Even when it was agony.' She winced and lapsed into silence again and Rudi decided she was far away, in another world, another decade, trawling the memories of a long-distant past.

He waited, and then, when he could wait no longer, he prompted, 'And so . . .'

She started, then looked at him with faintly malicious eyes. 'Oh yes. I've got to sing for my supper, haven't I?' She drained the last of her drink. Stung, he protested.

'No, no. Of course not. We can talk about anything you like.' But they both knew he was lying.

With a resigned sigh she took up the story again.

'That part of it is easy to tell,' she said. 'Now comes the difficult bit.'

'If you don't want to—' he began but she waved an imperious hand and continued.

'One night—one evening—I was in bed in my home in Malibu. There came a knocking, first at the front door, then at my bedroom door. I was alarmed. Although security was not the priority it is today—it was a much safer time—nevertheless for someone to get to my

56

*bedroom* door without my being informed was alarming.' She paused again and this time Rudi prompted her instantly.

'Who was it?' he asked breathlessly.

'The Feds,' she told him calmly. 'They'd come to arrest my lover. Well, not *arrest* him as such. *Remove* him, they said, at the request of their good friend Her Britannic Majesty of England.' She glanced up at him. 'Take him away. Deport him.' Tears began to fill the huge violet eyes, sprinkling them with stars. 'I was devastated. One moment he was there, in my life, the next whisked silently away. Disappeared into the night. I held onto him but he seemed resigned. Kissed me lightly and went. It was strange,' she told him. 'Extraordinary. They came in and went with him taking him with them, and then nothing. Not a word in the papers. Nothing. It was as if he had been a dream.

'I found out then that I was pregnant. I thought at first it was the shock of his abduction that stopped my period, but I was expecting his child. I knew the studio would force me to have an abortion or say the baby was Brent's, born in holy wedlock. That was essential. I knew Brent would go along with whatever was demanded. He was completely in their hands. He would have sold himself to the devil to maintain his status as the studio's top box office draw.' She smiled bitterly. 'If they'd pushed him he might even have given up his incessant romps with teenagers, bobbysocksers, but they thought he'd not be able to perform on-screen unless he had all that self-indulgence off-screen.

'I tried to find out what had happened to my lover. They said he was a gangster. You ever hear the like! Jimmy Cagney, "you dirty rat", now that I understand. Bogart, sure. But my lover? It was incongruous. Who ever heard of a gangster with an English accent?' She peered at Rudi. 'Did I say he was English? I guess not. But English in those days was upper class. Dignified toffs. Arcane elitism. Ronald Coleman and Leslie Howard. Gentlemen. Greer Garson and Merle Oberon. Ladies. But English gangsters? It seemed utterly bizarre. But then, my lover did not talk posh but he was certainly British. Spoke softly. Huskily. Of course I had not read Graham Greene or heard about the Kray twins or Mad Frankie Fraser. I was incredulous, distraught, seeing plots everywhere, becoming paranoid. It wasn't as crazy as it sounds. The studio was not above spying, removing unwanted people. They had a lot to lose.' She giggled. 'I cost them millions in the end,' she said smiling evilly to herself. 'But oh, how painful it was. Never had my feelings been so raw.'

The lights had been lowered and there was an even deeper hush over the lounge and foyer of the hotel. Rudi could see the glow of the desk lights over the reception area, little amber pools. The sleepy minion there was dozing over a *France-Dimanche*. A bell-boy sat on the edge of an ornate gilt chair behind a mottled marble pillar, his hands clasped loosely between his knees, his head drooping wearily over them, waiting, which was what the staff and servants here did a lot of the time. Wait.

'You see, I'd known little happiness in my life. I was only twenty-one. I'd been born in New York's Hell's Kitchen. My mother was always tired, my father working all the hours God sent. They were Polish. They'd run away from the war. Got out just ahead of Hitler's jack-booted army. They left everything behind. Money, position, a quiet, cultured life, to toil and stress in an alien place among strangers. No, there was not much to laugh about and ours was a gloomy household. My father had been an actuary but he spoke little English and no one would employ him at that work with his limited vocabulary so he ended up a plumber. He'd always been able to fix things so that's what he did in this new land. Oh Rudi, it's a common story. Unoriginal. He was angry, angry at the Germans whom he hated, angry at the Americans who would not recognise his worth, his credentials and he took it out on us. We paid.' She darted a swift glance at Rudi as if she guessed what was on his mind. 'No. He never laid a finger on us but his mood was always black. Deep, dark depression and it

59

weighed heavily on my mother. She never smiled or laughed.

'So I ran away. To Hollywood. Like thousands of others, in search of a dream. And I found success. I was one of the lucky ones and believe me we are in the minority. But I, having nothing to lose, fought savagely to "make it", as they say. Young people nowadays have such a constipated view of life. They mistake disillusionment for tragedy and getting what they want with no effort at all for passion. They rummage through the trauma of growing up far too soon, trying to find a reason, an explanation for their bewilderment, when it is, quite simply, a common symptom of growth. An upsurge of hormones. We just got on with it. They blame their parents, believing their parents should provide them with answers, as if they should know the answers of that particular time. They don't understand they have to make their own mistakes, fight their own battles, carve out their own destiny. I simply presented myself with relentless tenacity and finally got bit parts. Then Carla Merrydown, the all-American girl, the studio's hottest property got syphilis and had to disappear off the scene. They searched frantically for a replacement. I thrust myself under their noses with awful determination and the rest is history. I was eighteen and Brent Charles was my leading man. Our first movie together—*Where Love Is*—was a box office smash. The critics said we were dynamite together. "Charles 'n' Reine, Together 'n' Terrific" was bannered across the world in letters high as a skyscraper. It was heady stuff.

'He seduced me of course, then the studios—who were worried about his sexual exploits—thought, wouldn't it be a great idea if he married me. I would be a stabilising influence on him and at worst they could cover up his indiscretions by releasing publicity shots of us, ecstatic in each other's arms, denying point blank the rumours of his infidelities as malicious gossip. The policy of VIPs worldwide. Deny everything. The American Way.

'I didn't know anything of this,' she told him. 'I was green. Helpless in their hands. Mind you, I don't think it would have made any difference if I *had* known. I would still have married him. I said a happy yes when Brent proposed.' She shook her head slowly, marvelling at her own words. 'I was so foolish, so young! Oh, to be that age again and to know what I know now!

'So you see, when the English gangster came on the scene I was ripe for plucking. Ready, as they say, to fall into his lap.

'I followed him to London. That was a mistake, but I was pregnant and frightened. I left Brent and the studios without a thought. You know the scenario, Rudi: escaping in a

61

scarf, huge dark glasses, only my maid with me. Just up and went, leaving the film unfinished. Like Schubert. Unfinished Symphony.' She laughed—mirthlessly, Rudi thought. 'I was in for a very hard time. A time, dear boy, of disaster and despair.' She shuddered and held out her glass. 'Get me another brandy, there's a dear. I need it for this bit.'

Rudi did as he was told, ringing for a waiter, ordering, waiting impatiently for the drinks to come, trying to appear relaxed.

When she'd had a few sips of the brandy she continued.

'London was horrible. I'd never been there before and coming from California was a culture shock. The city had not yet recovered from the bombing and although it was being rebuilt the destruction caused by the Luftwaffe was very much part of the dismal, dilapidated scene. It was cold and gloomy and depressing. I had left a golden, opulent world of sun and sand and blue seas and skies and come to this grey, dismal, claustrophic place and I was very unhappy. My vision too was coloured by my state of mind, my lost love.

'And I could not find him. I searched endlessly. People were evasive and noncommittal about him, downright furtive at the sound of his name. They shied away like frightened animals when I asked. I met blank denial about him everywhere and I went from place to place, joint to joint in Soho, searching, searching, searching. But never finding him and getting this odd reaction when I mentioned his name.

The studios were furious with me and I can't say that I blamed them. They froze all my assets, my money. They owned me lock, stock and barrel and I found myself penniless. Any savings I had they froze, setting what my disappearance cost against them.

'No one wanted me. I was blacklisted. The word was out. Use Nola Reine at your peril. And if by any chance you were crazy enough to employ her, any film with Nola Reine in it would not get distributed. There is no fury like a studio scorned, believe you me.

'I lost the baby, and that was the saddest thing. I was heartbroken.

'I took a dancing job in Raymond's Review Bar. It was not too bad. Not sleazy like some.' She glanced at him. 'Not swish either,' she added.

'Didn't anyone recognise you?' Rudi asked. She nodded.

'Oh yes. But they thought they'd made a mistake. I was so drab. The light had gone out inside me, all my vitality snuffed out.

'You can see I'm small. Up there on the screen I looked larger than life. The film star, groomed, gilded, exquisitely gowned and made up; my screen image, touched up, prepared, had gone. Vanished—and there was only a little mouse in my place. I had, you see, feet of clay. I'd come down off the pedestal of the goddess and I looked very ordinary, just like everyone else—and they didn't like that. Oh, they thought, she's *like* Nola Reine, but no, this anxious defeated dancer could not possibly be that shining star.

'Some guessed the truth. They read the papers and put two and two together. The ones who knew shied away from me, as if failure was contagious. Also I had said I wanted to get in touch with Victor Sandar, murderer, gangster, man of fear—'

'It was he?'

'Oh yes. It was he and it was not healthy to be connected with him.' She paused, took another swallow of her drink, lit another Gauloise. 'I eventually heard he was in Spain. Marbella. It was underdeveloped territory then. Not the exclusive spot it is now. It was in a magazine I came across. Photographs of him, a bit blurred, shying away from the camera; you could see he didn't want to be photographed, a vicious expression on his face. The article was outraged by his freedom. "This murderer suns himself in luxury while his victims and their families suffer the tortures of the damned, yet they are innocent victims whose only crime was to cross this villain's path."

'I had to acknowledge, finally, that it was all true. Read up about his life of crime yourself,

Rudi, for I'll not tell you tonight. I can't go into it, it's too painful. But don't judge me, Rudi. His guilt shows just how innocent I was, how duped. How foolish.'

She had slumped down in the wheelchair and remained as if exhausted.

His heart was touched and he said, 'I'd never judge you, Nola.'

She pushed herself up by her arms and straightened her shoulders as if bracing herself. 'I never saw him again,' she said tiredly. 'Until tonight. Never laid eyes on him since that night he was arrested in my bedroom in Malibu.'

'You didn't go to Spain? Didn't try to—'

'Of course I did! What do you think? I saved, got a flight to Malaga, hitched up the costa to Marbella. But he wouldn't see me. I climbed over the walls of his villa but his gorillas threw me out.'

'Maybe he didn't know it was you.'

'Oh, he knew! I wrote. Sent messages. Phoned. Once on the phone I heard the servant call out, "Signor, a lady, Nola Reine, to speak with you," and I heard his voice, unmistakable, "Tell 'er I'm out. Not here, Juan."

'I gave up eventually. I got tired of crawling, humbling myself, begging this thug to see me. I had demeaned myself enough. It was over. I and my love were worn out. Kaput.'

'How did he get from the USA to Malaga,

65

Nola? After all, he was arrested and deported.'

'Yes! He was deported, sent to trial at the Old Bailey. But the witnesses all changed their stories. Some disappeared. They could not, as the saying goes, pin anything on him. He left England though. There were eyes everywhere and enemies, so he eventually settled here. In France.'

'And you, Nola? How did you come to—'

'I went one day to the bar in the hotel I stayed at in Malaga. I had landed myself a job there as a *chanteuse*. Singing torch songs: "Along came Bill", "Stormy Weather"—you know. I have to admit I wasn't much good. However, I had one admirer. As I say, I was in the bar treating myself to a champagne cocktail and there was this little man who came up and sat beside me. He introduced himself, the Comte of a country long since gone, Theophile de Sevigné. French, but only derived from there in the nineteenth century. Minor nobility, like most of the titles here. He told me he adored my singing. Then he told me he adored me. He had perfect manners and merry eyes.' She smiled fondly as one would at the thought of a beloved child, or dog, or cat. 'I didn't fall in love with him,' she added. 'There was no overwhelming passion as there had been with Victor Sandar. But he was fun. He knew how to enjoy life and he adored me. You know, Rudi, I never regretted our marriage. Not for a moment. I gave him good value and together we enjoyed ourselves enormously.

'People, the gossips, the cynics, the *jealous* said I married him for his money. But,' she rolled her eyes, 'they were wrong. Thing was, unlike a lot of the titles racketing along the coast, he *had* made a pile for himself, investing wisely. Of course it helped. Without it he would not have been the man I so much admired, who took me to grand places and provided me with a luxurious and comfortable life. But I married him because he made me laugh and we had a good time together. Light-hearted times. Out of Greek tragedy and into Noel Coward. I'd had enough of clawing my way through the darker side of life.'

'Did you ever return to America?'

She shook her head vehemently. 'No. Never. Unlike Bergman—who was, unlike me, a *real* actress—I never went back. Did not desire to. Couldn't bear to revisit the scene of my downfall. Stir those memories.' She blew a cloud of blue smoke towards the cherubs on the ceiling. 'Brent is still around,' she said.

Rudi nodded. 'I know,' he replied.

'He's married a little teenager called Desiree Lamour. Last year. In his seventieth. Can you believe?' He didn't contradict her. Desiree was in her middle twenties but it was not worth quibbling over. 'He's had two face-lifts that I know of and his cheeks are pumped full of collagen. Yet he seems happy enough. I reckon it's because his heart is in his crotch and that makes everything easy.'

'Do you keep in touch?'

'Holy mackerel, no! I haven't seen him since the night before I left Hollywood. He'd be horrified if he saw me. As I said, I'd remind him of his mortality and that would never do.'

'So, when you saw Victor Sandar tonight, how did you feel?'

'My heart near jumped out of my chest. I felt I was going to suffocate. Oh, I'd known he was here but he rarely goes out. He doesn't socialise. His wife does. Cynthia. Poor woman. And I'm only here for a month each summer. I spend the rest of my time in Paris. The most beautiful city in the world.'

'So your heart jumped . . . and then?' Rudi persisted. He wanted to know.

'Then it returned to normal. I looked at him and wondered what I ever saw. Everything passes, Rudi. Sadly, everything passes. He was, after all, an old man with a leathery face and cold and hard eyes.' Then an infinitely sad expression suffused her eyes and her voice shook. 'Oh God, how I wish I hadn't wasted so much time yearning for him. Wasted. All wasted.'

She looked at Rudi, silently shaking her head from side to side. 'So much wasted time! So many hours, days, months, years. Wet pillows, boxes of tissues, an aching heart, agonising, yearning, for what? For a wicked,

wicked heartless man not worthy of the time I gave him in my head.' She sighed. 'Love, Rudi, is a strange and unpredictable emotion. It's so arbitrary. It alights haphazardly, where it will, on this person or that, spreading poison into your very soul. Like a virus it will not go, takes hold, blinds you. And it does not let go, holds on tenaciously until, sometimes, it is too late. One's life has flown past leaving one barren. Or it goes. Vanishes suddenly and the other is left bewildered by the desertion. Why? What happened? How come you loved me yesterday and today you are indifferent to my pain? Oh, it is a cunning emotion. Evil.'

'You are tired.' Rudi stated the obvious. She nodded.

'Yes. The thrill has gone out of the night, Rudi, and we, regretfully, must part.'

'I'll take you home.'

'Thank you.' She leaned forward suddenly and plucked his sleeve. 'But Rudi, be careful. You don't stand a chance. With his daughter, I mean. You know that. Don't you? Better watch out. Victor Sandar is a very dangerous man and Alice is the light of his life. So I'm warning you. Learn from my experience and beware.'

# CHAPTER EIGHT

'Where is she? Where is she?' Victor Sandar's urgent voice preceded him into the villa.

The graceful woman sitting there had no need to ask whose whereabouts was sought. Cynthia Sandar was well aware that there was no one other than his daughter, Alice, who could so excite her husband.

'She's in bed,' she told him calmly. 'Asleep.'

He had burst into the house, eyes distracted and he looked at her now with something like hatred.

'Are you sure? Some young man next door said—'

Cynthia sighed theatrically, rose and called out, 'Nana. Nana.' The woman answered almost immediately from above. 'Yes missus?'

'Is Alice in bed?'

'Yes, missus.' Nana was leaning over the wrought-iron banisters. 'Hush up or you'll wake her.'

'Mr Sandar wants you to check.'

Nana threw a glance up to heaven. 'I just *been* there!' she protested.

'Don't be cheeky, Nana,' Cynthia instructed patiently. 'Check again, there's a dear.'

The face withdrew and disappeared, to reappear moments later crying triumphantly, '*Yes*. She's there. Safely tucked up.' Then, with an aggressive upturn to her voice, 'Okay?'

Cynthia nodded and returned to the chair where she'd been sitting before her husband burst in. Picking up her book, she began to read.

'Someone made a remark next door,' Victor Sandar said again, by way of explanation. 'Said a friend of that ass Jonathan had her, had Alice. Was with her.'

'Would that have been so bad?' Cynthia asked mildly.

'He's a bleeding jerk. They all are.'

'Jonathan? I suppose. His chum mightn't be though. Might be a nice friend for Alice.'

Victor strode over to his wife and with one violent but controlled swipe knocked the book viciously out of her hands. She did not move, showed no emotion, remained where she was, unflinching, staring at the book on the floor.

'Don't you ever listen?' he asked, tight-mouthed. 'I will not have my daughter associating with such . . .'

She didn't bother to reply. She knew he wanted a fight, an excuse to be abusive to her because he was so riled up. I'll not give him one, she thought, so she said nothing.

The ground floor of the villa was all one big open space, marble-floored with locally woven rugs scattered about. The ornaments too were Provençal, the sofas and armchairs were covered in cobalt blue and blue glass and lampshades gave the room an almost Greek

71

ambience. The staircase which swam gracefully into the middle of the room led up to the bedrooms and Victor Sandar's study. Not that there was anything actually *in* his study. Victor Sandar was not a man who burdened himself with paperwork, records or files of any sort.

The main living area where Cynthia was sitting opened out onto the swimming pool and terrace at one end, the front entrance at the other.

When Victor Sandar had left the Crawley's villa, above them and to the west side, he had run the quarter-mile down home and burst in through the front door demanding to know where his daughter was. Cynthia watched him as she might have stared at an insect she'd come across unexpectedly on her bathroom floor. She had tried to catch a glimpse of his eyes. Those eyes! They were either cold as the north wind or smouldering dangerously with a wild, almost insane intent. Neither expression boded well.

Not that Cynthia was worried. She knew he would not harm her. She was Alice's mother and therefore sacred. Not because he respected the maternal role but because Alice adored her and to keep Alice happy was the passionate aim of Victor Sandar's life. Upsetting Alice and the resultant threat that she might be angry with him was his constant fear. His other great fear was that she might learn the truth about him.

Cynthia stared at him across the room. He was a good-looking man with a hatchet face too used to the sun, a man who reeked of latent vitality and suppressed violence. He was a ruthless and cruel man with, she reflected, one glaring weakness: his adoration of his daughter.

She was terrified of the undertow of his thoughts and actions and she had married him because she had been terrified not to. She knew that there was nowhere she could hide from him and that he always got what he wanted.

And he had wanted her. He had wooed her, this woman of society, this Roedean-educated, upper class but penniless lady, wooed her with displays of wealth that dazzled her and a sexual prowess that enslaved her. After that meeting at a party in Monte Carlo she had been lost to common sense, to dignity, to freedom.

They had played a game ever since, a game based in the fantasy that they were like other people. A battle of class and sex, a duel of opposites which excited and angered them both. Before Alice's birth Cynthia had always lost but after Alice's arrival she often won.

The game they played was based on hatred and resentment and they both enjoyed it though either would have admitted it, were perhaps not even aware of it. He sharpened his

73

teeth subduing her, displaying his power over her, defeating her and trying to prove the 'common man's' superior strength, sharpness and ability to succeed which, he believed, the more intellectual upper classes lacked miserably when they attempted to carve out an empire. 'Without the gun of poverty in your back there is no impetus,' he would say.

She on the other hand enjoyed highlighting his ignorance, his lack of social nicety, her intellectual superiority and her ability to face his rages with equanimity. 'Intelligent people don't lose control,' she'd told him once serenely, when his hand was inches from her face. 'Only fools!' And she'd watched with delight his struggle with himself. He'd backed down, dropping his hand in comedic fashion, first rubbing his face, then fumbling, trying to place it in his jacket pocket, pretending he had not been going to do what he obviously wanted to do.

There was nothing she enjoyed more than to defeat him with a clever sentence, see him squirm when he committed a gaffe in front of others.

After Alice's birth she slowly became aware of the power that being her mother gave her. An immense power over him. Once, only once he'd shouted viciously at her in their daughter's presence and Alice had burst into tears and would not be consoled until he'd apologised (which he'd loathed doing) and they'd kissed and made up. Cynthia smiled at the memory. Little Alice, all of six years old, begging him to say sorry. 'I do if I'm naughty.' Her little face had been indignant but trusting him to do the right thing.

'I've said I'm sorry, pet, to you.'

'No, no, Dadda. You must say sorry to Mamma.'

He had. That was how much he adored his child.

'What are you smiling at?' he asked now, pouring himself a whisky, mollified now he'd reassured himself that Alice was tucked up safely in bed.

'Oh, nothing.' She bent, picked up her book, but closed it and laid it on the small table beside her chair in a smooth graceful gesture. She was the epitome of understated elegance. Her natural blond hair lay in a shining pageboy bob framing the classical features her daughter had inherited. Her slim body was athletic and she wore a light silk Armani suit, casually cut in a soft biscuit colour, and a white silk shirt underneath.

'Did you enjoy the party?' she asked, coolly civilised. She could have been asking a stranger the question.

'No,' he replied. 'Brompton Crawley talked in my face the whole time. Stupid man!'

'Well, you *would* go.'

'I wanted to show them. Stick two fingers up. Bloody nerds. They keep me out of the

75

frigging country but are only too happy to have me as a dinner guest. Frig—'

'No need to use bad language.'

'I'll use whatever language I bloody well like.' It was an unheated, automatic reply.

She looked at him. 'You gave them my apologies? And Alice's?' He nodded. She hesitated a moment then said, 'Victor, she's going to have to be allowed out once in a while you know. You can't keep her locked up forever—the princess in the tower. We don't live in mediaeval times.' She wanted more than anything for Alice to have a normal, happy life. To fall in love, once, twice. Eventually to marry. 'She should go to the Princess's party on the weekend for instance.'

He swung around. 'I'll keep her locked up—as you call it—if I want. But she's not locked up. Is she? She's free to come and go as she pleases. You know that,' he fired at her.

'But only with us. With bodyguards who report to you,' she retorted. 'I'll be with her—'

'I can do anything I like with her,' he continued, not hearing what she said. 'She's mine, do you hear?'

'And mine,' she replied. If he loved Alice, so did she. But her love for her daughter was unselfish, not possessive. Cynthia would fight for her child's happiness.

'She's eighteen,' Cynthia went on. 'She wants to go to dances.'

'She *does* go,' he growled back. 'The

Princess's party—'

'With me! She wants to go to discos. With the young people.'

'Like Jonathan Crawley, you mean? Never! I wouldn't trust him as far as I'd throw him. You should have seen him tonight. Him and his friends. Idiots!'

'All young people are idiots, Victor. That's what youth is for. Being silly.'

'Not Alice. Over my dead body.'

'And that story about her life being in danger. She won't accept it much longer as a reason to be chaperoned everywhere. Or else you'll have to tell her the real reason.'

'Do you want to end up—' He was raging. She knew that yet she did not seem to be able to stop herself.

'Killed? Murdered? Oh come now, Victor . . .'

'There's a contract out on my life. Everyone knows it.

'It should not affect Alice.'

'Well, it does. Anyone close to me is a target.' She shivered. 'And well you know it. You simply choose to ignore it. Typical bloody elitist attitude.'

'Do you want her to grow to hate you?' Cynthia asked. She'd hit a nerve and she knew it. He winced.

'She'll never hate me. She adores me,' he said.

'If you keep her prisoner she will.'

'I told you. She's *mine.* I'll do whatever I want.'

'Then you'll lose her. Inevitably.' It was a statement brooking no argument.

He looked across the room at her. 'Never, you hear me, *never* threaten me like that again.' He spoke softly, menacingly. She stared back into his eyes, unblinking.

'I sometimes think you married me to sire her exclusively for yourself,' she said quietly. He recoiled in disbelief, staring at her silently. His eyes had their graveyard expression. Then he relaxed suddenly and shrugged.

'Exactly,' he agreed. 'Exactly.' Then he added gently, 'Remember that.'

'So you intend to keep her all to yourself.' She persisted in spite of his warning glance. They had never before been down this road. 'As what?' she queried. 'A prisoner? A slave? Until she's an old maid?' She drew in a sharp breath. 'Or as a mistress?' she whispered.

Watching his face she was suddenly very frightened. He had gone pale under his tan. A white line appeared around his lips and he sucked in his breath sharply through his teeth. All his emotions were there writ large for her to read. She could see that the thought had not really occurred to him before and his face was a battleground of conflicting violent emotions.

'That's it, isn't it?' she cried, unable to stop herself. 'Eventually it's out in the open. You desire your own daughter! You want to seduce her but you dare not! Oh my God in heaven. She'd hate you if she knew. She'd detest you if she got even a glimpse of what's in your sick head. You'd poison her love for you forever and you know it.' She laughed harshly. 'Oh, what a cleft stick you are in, Victor! I pity you.' He tried to speak but choked on his words. She stared at him. 'God have mercy on you, Victor.' She was almost crying. 'You want her for yourself and given half a chance you'd do it. But you dare not for she'd turn from you in disgust and loathing. It's what keeps you restless, isn't it? Keeps you tossing and turning at night. Not the contract out on you. You don't really think that's a possibility. And not the fact that a great number of people want you dead. No. Your lust for your daughter is what makes you uneasy, makes your spirit unquiet.' She continued relentlessly, seizing onto this Achilles heel. 'You are a disgusting man, a pathetic excuse for a man.'

'Shut up, woman. Shut up. Keep your filthy thoughts to yourself,' he snarled at her.

'But this is the 1990s,' she cried. 'We live in enlightened times. She's not a poor innocent that could be persuaded Daddy was within his rights. That it was an okay thing to do. A perfectly normal thing in fact. You can't do that, can you? She's seen Oprah and Ricki Lake. She's watched Esther Rantzen and she knows about Child Line and all that. She's read the books, the magazines, been part of a crusade at school to help victims of abuse. The convent,' she spat at him. 'The all-girls school you insisted she go to has enlightened her for her protection.' She was shaking now, her usually calm features twisted and angry. 'She knows too much for you to corrupt her, Victor.'

He would have killed her then, could have slowly cut her up and watched her die as he'd watched others die, glad that they suffered. His hatred bubbled like molten lead, like a volcano flooding his brain. All the things he'd married her for now irritated him intensely. Her cleverness, her upper class poise, her cool, perfect, ladylike manners. He put his hands to his head and cried out, 'Shut up, shut up, shut up, you lying bitch. Never, never make such a filthy suggestion again. You are twisted, you know that? You are jealous, that's what it is. She loves me and you hate that—'

'Mummy? Daddy?'

She stood there at the top of the stairs leaning over the banister in her long lawn nightdress, her shining hair tousled, her eyes full of sleep.

'Daddy, you woke me up. What is it? Shouting . . .'

He stood, but it was Cynthia who moved towards her daughter. 'It's nothing, sweetheart,' she said, her voice placating, calm. 'Nothing at all.'

'I heard shouting.'

'It was a dream, sweetheart. Daddy and I were having an argument. You know how we do, sometimes. It's nothing, pet. Back to bed now.' She ran up the stairs and put her arm around her daughter's shoulders. 'Come to bed, dearest. Come to bed.'

She led the drowsy girl back to her bedroom. Before they went into her room Cynthia glanced over her shoulder down at her husband standing at the foot of the stairs and for a moment she was sorry for him. She'd never seen this expression on his face before. His shoulders drooped and his eyes were battlegrounds of anger and pain. He looked bewildered, the perplexed expression on his face revealing his inner turmoil. Cynthia realised he'd never wanted to face this, wanted things to go on as they were, unsaid. He wanted to continue cosseting his beloved, showering her with his love, presents, showing her off, basking in her beauty, hugging her, kissing her. Oh God. But time would not stand still. Alice was maturing. The kissing would have to stop. Alice would want to meet a young man her own age, find love.

Cynthia was glad she had forced him tonight to acknowledge his feelings, face the reality against his will. Let him wriggle out of that one, she thought. It would checkmate him. There was no way now that anything could happen 'accidentally'. No way he could plead ignorance. This fact would drive him crazy.

Cynthia shivered. His dark impulses were laid bare and he'd never forgive her. He'd find a way to make her suffer. But what did that matter if her beloved Alice was happy?

It would be healthier; the light of her knowledge beamed on the situation would give him pause. There could now be no inadvertant or impulsive happening. She'd seen to that. Alice was safe.

The girl smelled of wild herb shampoo and Cynthia buried her face in her daughter's tangle of hair, kissing the sweet-scented waves. She could understand Victor's feeling and she shuddered again at the shocking thought.

Alice's eyelids were drooping and she curled up as Cynthia pulled the coverlet over her.

'Night, sweetheart.'

'Night, Mummy,' came the murmured reply.

Cynthia went softly to the door. She thought she heard something, something her daughter muttered in her sleep. She turned.

'Sweetheart? What is it?' But Alice's eyes were fast closed.

'Rudi. Oh Rudi,' she whispered and slid into deep unconsciousness, leaving her mother standing in the doorway.

Rudi?

# CHAPTER NINE

The boy stood in the sparsely furnished room in an ancient house tucked behind a crumbling old building way behind the Croisette. Though not too far from the glamorous hotels on the front it was a million miles away in style and comfort.

The room was quite clean, though like a monk's cell with its linoleum-covered floor and functional furniture. A bed, like a hospital bed—a cot, really—with a white candlewick spread was pushed against one wall. There was an ancient enamel basin and a pitcher full of lukewarm water on a rickety stand on the other side. A curtain was drawn across a row of hangers for clothes and a chest of drawers and nothing else.

The room faced north and the sun was a stranger here which may have been why the boy had so easily been able to rent it despite the fact that it was high season on the Côte d'Azur.

He was sweating. There was no air-conditioning, not even a ceiling fan to move the turgid air around a bit. His tee shirt clung to him and there was a dark pyramid-shaped stain on the back where it stuck to his body. He wore jeans and Nike sneakers and his hair hung over his eyes as he cleaned his long-barrelled revolver.

He pulled back the hammer, his concentration never wavering. He had bought the Colt in a little shop in Paris. It had been much easier than he had anticipated. He sat there cleaning, caressing it lovingly in the silence of the room.

He was a good-looking boy but nondescript. A neat nose, thick chestnut hair, nice teeth, but his dark eyes were shuttered, closing out everyday communication with his fellow human beings. His eyes dwelt somewhere else, in another space.

He was a boy with a purpose, an aim. An eighteen-year-old with the closed mind and the confused feelings of most chaps his age. But unlike the many he was single-minded, focused on his task.

The journey had been tiring. He'd been scared all the time. He had been quite sure everyone, all the officials, particularly those at passport control, could read his mind, could see murder in his eyes.

He'd never been out of England before and could not understand a word of French. He was sure when they jabbered to each other that they were talking about him. He didn't like the food. It upset his already nervous stomach. But he was consumed by the mission he was on and did not allow such minor disturbances to get to him. Like a knight of old in pursuit of the Holy Grail, determinedly blinkered, he ploughed on. Everything that irritated or hampered him was a triviality.

He'd caught the train at Waterloo. It was packed. He wondered when he'd see England again. Perhaps never.

He was going to commit murder. They'd be after him on his return journey, if he was not caught before then—at the scene of the crime for instance. They'd be hunting him if he did succeed in fleeing. He'd be a fugitive.

How could he plan an escape before he knew what the terrain was like? How could he plan to duck and dive to avoid the *gendarmes* when he was a stranger to the territory? Oh, he had a return ticket but would he be able to use it? He'd probably be caught. He half hoped he would be. It would make banner headlines in the *Sun,* the *Express* and the *Mirror*. It might even rate a more discreetly worded front page paragraph in the *Guardian,* the *Independent, The Times.*

And everyone in England would be on his side. Cheering. Even the police, maybe *especially* the police would be sympathetic towards him. DO Beresford would celebrate. But he'd be in France. Would they extradite him? he wondered. He hoped so.

He could visualize the headlines. 'Son of murdered baker caught at Gare du Nord.' 'Son of Grantley Sloane sought vengeance. Shot the man who murdered his father.' And the more temperate papers: 'Martin Sloane, whose

father, Grantley Sloane, was allegedly tortured and killed by Victor Sandar fifteen years ago, was caught today trying to board a train in Paris carrying the gun with which he alleges he executed the man he holds responsible for his father's murder. "I could not rest until the man who killed my father was dead or behind bars," Martin said as they handcuffed him.'
And, 'East End gangster Victor Sandar who fled London with what is reputed to have been a fortune was living quietly in the South of France with his wife, the former Lady Cynthia Maine-Harrington and his daughter, Alice. He denied any connection with the London underworld and police failed to link him with the crimes he allegedly committed. No proof was ever found to connect him with the murders and he had cast-iron alibis for the times they were supposed to have been committed.'

No proof! No proof! Martin's mother had *seen* it. She had been there, actually present when Victor Sandar had forced her to watch while he tortured and killed her husband before her very eyes.

But she'd been too afraid to testify against him. Victor Sandar's arm was long and he had told her that if she 'grassed him up' young Martin would be the next to go. She dared not take the risk. She had told Martin, 'I wanted to, so bad, but I knew he'd kill you and you're all I've got now your Da has gone.'

Victor Sandar still ruled from his villa in France. Martin knew that because his henchmen had never loosed their hold on his mother. Only last month two of his heavies had barged into their home, paying them the token visit they made every so often, to remind the Sloanes, Eddy the Ferret told them often enough, to keep their traps shut. Smiling broadly they invited themselves in. There were always two of them. Big bullies, Martin had discovered, never went anywhere alone. Eddie brought a different sidekick each time. This time Eddie and a scrawny teenager with a shaved head and angry eyes obviously eager for a fight arrived and demanded afternoon tea.

Martin watched his mother prepare the meal with trembling hands, terrified of angering them, doing her 'yes sir' 'no sir' bit, subserviently bowing and scraping to the thugs who protected the man who had killed her husband, his father. They grinned at her, enjoying her humiliation.

'A message from France,' the one with the feral teeth—Eddie the Ferret—told her. 'You're not forgotten. You don't want nothin' happenin' to you pretty face. Or 'im,' he had jerked his head towards Martin. 'Could do IRA stuff on 'im. Knee-cap,' and he laughed, his lips pulling back over those terrible Dracula teeth and crimson gums.

Eddie the Ferret found things out, kept

things smooth for his boss. Travelled back and forth to France first class. Had money to burn, protection money taken from people like Martin's father. Eddie wore Armani suits and Gieves & Hawkes shirts and silk Italian ties and handmade shoes. Eddie liked to throw his weight about but never forgot who was boss. He wasn't clever enough to run the whole operation and was smart enough to be aware of that. He was unswervingly loyal to Victor Sandar.

Martin's father had made the mistake of standing up to Victor Sandar, refusing to pay protection. A baker with a sweet-smelling shop and a lovely wife and little boy, he had seen no reason to be held to ransom with the threat of force. The other traders had egged him on. Oh, they were all behind him in his fight until he was murdered. After that the whole area fell spinelessly into the maw of the gangster and his staff of hoodlums. Not a peep out of anyone after that. And his mother lived her life in abject fear.

Eddie had told them one day, casually, conversationally, that it was not meant to happen. 'It went a bit far, see. 'E was a stubborn cuss an' he wouldn't agree. Just wouldn't give in. We 'ad to show 'im who was boss.'

Martin had asked the police to wire him but they explained very kindly that a tape on which Eddie said something incriminating about

Victor Sandar would not put him behind bars. There was nothing they could do.

Martin was in a lather that last day when they came to tea in case they turned the house over. They often did. Ransacked it. Looking for what? He did not know. Maybe a tape. Maybe they did not know it would not be enough to have their boss banged up. Maybe they did it just for the hell of it. But on that occasion he was terrified they'd find his passport. He had just got it, brand new. And they didn't know he had it. They'd specified that the Sloanes were not to leave London. If they found he had a passport he did not know what would happen.

But they didn't. They'd become complacent. They did not for a moment imagine the Sloanes would disobey orders. They were used to the habit of obedience.

They drank their tea, ate the scones and small neat sandwiches his mother had made. Once, when he was about ten years old, his mother had left the crusts on the sandwiches and Eddie had lost his cool and screamed at her, dashing the plate onto the floor, spilling egg and cress and cucumber everywhere. 'You think I'm scum, don't you? Well I'm as good as anyone, just like your dad. Remember that. You better treat me right or you're dead meat.'

Martin wet his trousers, standing there, petrified. It seemed to him that Eddie the Ferret grew and grew and grew, towering over his little mother. And Eddie's name was terror.

His mother had been sick for a month after that episode. She'd never forgotten to cut the crusts off Eddie the Ferret's sarnies again.

Martin blinked away the tears that stung the back of his eyes as he stood in the little room in France. He must not give in to sentiment now. The time to cry had not yet come.

He had always wanted revenge. The reason he'd not made this journey before, come to France, shot the bastard was because of what Eddie might do to his mother in his absence. The thought made him turn cold. She only had him to protect her from them.

Then, a month ago, his mother had suffered a stroke. She was recovering nicely and was very cheerful because she was in hospital and no one could get at her there. Her stroke had been caused by Victor Sandar and his men, Martin knew that. She'd spent fifteen years in a blue funk and that took its toll. So the one person Martin loved was running out of strength. And she was out of harm's way, safely in the hospital. They wouldn't risk doing anything there. Victor Sandar did not take chances. Hospitals had surveillance nowadays and who knew what the cameras might pick up? He had to act now—while she was safe—or he'd procrastinate forever. The time was right. God given.

So he'd meticulously planned this assassination, for there was no way he could rid himself of Victor Sandar except by killing him.

Oh, he could run away, himself and his mother, like criminals. They'd talked about it often enough. Go to some remote island in the China Sea or emigrate to New Delhi, or journey to some isolated island in Alaska. But they would never be free. They would be exiled, isolated, still frightened—for what guarantee had they that some day Victor Sandar or his men would not catch up with them?

No, there was only one way, Martin decided, and that was to eliminate the man he hated, the man with the power. Martin was clever enough to work out that Eddie the Ferret had no ambitions to take over Victor Sandar's empire. If he or any of his henchmen in the organisation aimed that high they'd have made their move long ago. Sandar had been living abroad long enough now for it to be obvious that no one in London was going to dispute his leadership. He ran a smooth relentless operation from wherever he was and it seemed none of his enforcers had ambitions to oust him. No, Martin figured, none of them so far had had the bottle.

This was both a bad thing and a good thing for Martin. It was bad in so far that as long as Victor Sandar remained in control his life and his mother's were under threat. He'd have to pay and pay, submit to the terror of those visits, locked in an invisible prison. The good part was that when Victor Sandar died the threat was automatically gone, the reign of terror would be over. No opposing power would care whether Martin grassed or not. In fact, it would probably suit them if Martin did. Discredit Victor Sandar. New broom sweeps clean.

Martin sat on the wicker chair and stared out of the window. The shutters did not fold completely back and all he could see was the brick wall of the house next door. No misty blue vista here. No sweeping lawns, no soothing multi-green shades of pine and cedar, of willow and elm. No clusters of gaudy bougainvillea or hydrangea, no splashes of blinding blue wisteria or lavish displays of hibiscus. No murmur of the cobalt sea twisting and turning and heaving. No delicate chains of lights like gold necklaces along the coast. The views from the villas were not for Martin Sloane. Only a grey stone wall.

Not that he would have appreciated a view, however spectacular. He probably would not have seen it, not noticed it. He was too preoccupied with his thoughts. A man with only one idea in his head. To kill Victor Sandar.

He had not slept since he came to the South of France, but he was not tired. He lay wide awake, figuring, brooding, going over and over his plan. He snapped the cartridge back and laid the gun beside him as he lay there, touching it with one hand, the other palm upwards over his eyes, the record playing over and over in his head.


## CHAPTER TEN

Martin Sloane was not the only one who did not sleep that night. Rudi Wolfe sat at the table in his modest room, a room not much better than Martin's, and tried to scribble notes on his project. The magazine paid for the *pension* and, to give them credit, had offered to put him up in much more upmarket accommodation. However, Rudi liked to choose where he stayed and he preferred simplicity. He said it helped him concentrate his mind.

He was wide awake, alert, far from the exhaustion he usually felt at this time of the morning. Visions of the girl floated before his eyes, insinuating images of her loveliness between him and what he was trying to write. So eventually he too lay on his back and ruminated.

He had been through an emotional wringer in the war zone he had recently returned from. His visions until tonight had been the stuff of nightmares. Man's inhumanity to man appalled him and his brain had been clouded

93

by bitter speculation, pictures of the horrors he had seen refusing to be banished, troubling his sleep, haunting his waking hours. Women and children in despair. Men's mangled bodies. Boys cut down before they had time to live, lying on the cold ground as if fast asleep only they were dead. Hunger. Starvation. Misery and blood. The drama of war sickened him, shocked him to the core. He was not a soldier, had not been indoctrinated. Unprepared for the mayhem, he had been at first disbelieving, then angered by what he saw.

How could any human being set this bloodbath in motion? What primeval territorial urge made it bearable for anyone to perpetrate such cruelty? There was no excuse for it, no ideology worth it.

Exhausted by the horror, Rudi had written his scorching article but the visions of war continued to haunt him, giving him no peace. He had accepted his state of mind, it became part of the fabric of his life.

*Newsdesk* had given him leave of absence, but it did not help. Messing about on his boat in Maine gave him no solace. It should have. It always had before. But in his isolation he had been haunted.

Then *Newsdesk* had sent him to France. The editor, an old friend, thought that work was probably the best cure for what ailed Rudi and Rudi had been glad enough to go to the South of France at the magazine's request.

He had still been plagued with nightmares.

Until tonight.

There were no haunted dreams tonight, there were no visions of horror, there was only her beauty, her grace. That lovely body moved in slow motion, bathed in its aquamarine glow like a golden statue come to life at the bottom of the Aegean Sea. He could visualise her every move, every ripple of muscle, every balletic arabesque, so graceful as she dived into the pool. The towel around her, her movement within the white sheath as she patted herself dry. Her face breaking the smooth water and emerging like a lily pad dewed with diamond drops of water, a goddess rising like Aphrodite from the foam. Standing on the balcony in her Victorian lawn and lace nightgown, her hair flowing out around that innocent, angelic face, that perfect alignment of bone, that inner glow that sparkled like champagne.

Oh, she was quite perfect, but that was not the whole. He had seen many a beauty in his journalistic life. When he'd done the article on Brent Charles he'd come across quite a few Hollywood stars who were stunning. He'd been at the Academy Awards and gasped at the parade of lovelies both famous and hopeful but there was something hard and determined about them all. Her face bore no marks of the struggles of life. It was utterly unscathed and the look of her gave him a body blow, made his heart beat out of control. It unmanned him, made him vulnerable as no one had ever done before.

Alice. Alice. He whispered her name in the dark as he lay on the bed, tossing and turning in the heat. As dawn broke over the Côte d'Azur he thought, Oh Alice, my love, my beautiful love, do you too dream of me? Or is that presumptuous? Are you unconscious on your pillow, your hair like a shower of gold around you, no thought in your head of the man you met in the tree tonight? Perhaps she had forgotten his existence. Perhaps. Perhaps.

However, she had not. Far away in her room in the *Villa Bella Vista* Alice was dreaming of him too. She smiled in her sleep and turned and sighed. Rudi.

As the first light of dawn pierced the shutters it made her stir. 'Oh, Rudi.' She whispered his name ardently.

And down the corridor Victor Sandar sat sleepless, heavy-eyed, brooding. He stared out unseeing over the pale sea, silver in the morning sun, and every now and then he hit the arm of his chair with his clenched fist.

'Never. Never. Never,' he muttered over and over again as his hand punched the chair arm furiously. 'Never. I'll kill her first.'

# CHAPTER ELEVEN

Rudi and Alice might not have met again if it had not been for Cynthia. Victor forbade his daughter to leave the villa.

'Why not, Daddy?' she asked, disappointment on her face.

'Because there are wicked men who want to harm us,' he told her.

'But Daddy . . .'

'No, Alice. You must do as I say. I know what's best for you. Trust me.'

She hung about the balcony and the pool searching the foliage for Rudi but he did not appear.

\*       \*       \*

He tried, God knows he tried, but the Crawleys had gone away for a couple of days on a friend's boat to Sardinia and there was no one at *Villa Beau Rivage*. All the alarms were on so Rudi could find no way in.

Jonathan had left him a note enclosing an invitation and saying they would be back in Antibes by the weekend. For the Princess's party.

'Hope you'll come. Ma would die rather than miss it. We'll all be there. Everyone. Even Victor Sandar and family! So do pitch up, old fellow. You don't know what a razzle I had to go through to get you this invite!'

\*          \*          \*

Rudi rang the front door of the Sandar villa. It was opened by a huge bodyguard, an evil-looking brute who told him that Miss Alice was not at home and slammed the door in his face.

\*          \*          \*

A few days later, Cynthia, in her daughter's bedroom, was trying to decide what Alice should wear for the Princess's party in Monte Carlo that night. Alice said she didn't care. She was obviously upset and disappointed about something and was showing no interest in her gown for the ball. So eventually Cynthia pulled her down beside her on the pale brocade chaise.

'Who is this Rudi?' she asked without preamble. The query had been hovering on her tongue for the last few days but she was loath to upset her daughter. She had heard about the young man who came every day and rang the bell and was refused entrance.

The room was awash with primrose sunshine and the vases everywhere were full of flowers. Alice looked at her mother apprehensively. 'How did you . . .' Her eyes were wide and questioning.

In the dressing-room off the bedroom Nana was pottering about and she leaned out holding up a delicate white beaded Valentino evening dress. 'This one I think, Ma'am. The sheath. Don't you?'

Cynthia looked up and nodded. 'I think that might very well do,' she said, smiling at Nana.

'It's got a tiny tear in the chiffon,' Nana told her. 'I'll mend it.' She went away and Cynthia looked quizzically back at her daughter and was surprised by the expression in her eyes. They were vibrant with passion, the velvet pupils enormous. Cynthia sucked in her breath. There was no mistaking it; her daughter was in love.

She looked heartrendingly lovely sitting in her satin rose-coloured bikini pants and bra. Her skin was smooth as the satin, as only an eighteen-year-old's could be, and she pushed her sheet of golden hair back from her face and looked at her mother anxiously.

'Oh Mummy, he's . . .'

'I know, pet, I know. He's the most wonderful man God ever put on the face of the earth. The handsomest, the most fabulous.'

Alice's eyes were wide. 'How did you know?' she asked. 'Because *every* girl's first love is.' Cynthia began to laugh.

'My *only* love,' Alice insisted.

'Well, as to that, we'll see.'

'Oh Mummy, I promise. He is—' she searched for a descriptive adjective that would do him justice and failed to find one.

'I believe you, sweetheart,' her mother said. 'But who is he?'

'Rudolph Wolfe is his name,' Alice breathed, 'Rudi. He's a friend of Jonathan Crawley. I met him the other night. He was in the tree. Out there.' She pointed out to the balcony laughing, her hand over her mouth, a habit she had since she wore braces. Cynthia automatically pulled her hand away. 'Don't do that,' she told her daughter mildly. 'Good Lord! In the tree?'

'Yes. In the Crawleys' villa. He's gorgeous, Mummy. He's . . . he's . . .' She petered out, unable to describe his perfection. She continued, 'We talked. Then he fell down out of the tree.' She laughed again, her hand travelling towards her mouth, Cynthia catching it when it was halfway there, holding it in hers. 'Nana was beside herself,' Alice continued, laughing.

'Nana knew?'

'Oh no! She thought I was talking to myself.' She collapsed in giggles and Cynthia was borne away on a tide of laughter with her daughter.

'I hope he didn't hurt himself?' Cynthia asked when their laughter had subsided. Her daughter's laugh was infectious, a bubble of pure mirth errupting from a well of joy deep inside her. 'Oh, please God don't let anything spoil her delight in life,' Cynthia prayed, thinking of her husband and trying to still her anxiety.

'I don't think so.' Alice suddenly looked troubled, all the sunshine wiped from her face. 'But Mummy, what . . . how—' They both knew she was thinking of her father. 'Will he be angry?' she stammered.

'Don't worry about Daddy for the moment, pet.' Cynthia screwed up her face, thinking. 'I'll get this Rudolph Wolfe invited to the party, the Princess's party. I don't think Daddy is going. He had enough of the Crawleys the other night. So I'll invite the Crawleys. And I'll deal with Daddy. But don't tell him, whatever you do, about this Rudi.'

Alice's face was troubled. 'I hate to deceive him,' she said. 'But why *shouldn't* I meet boys? Why should I have to lie? I'm old enough now.'

'You don't have to lie. Just don't say anything,' Cynthia told her.

'It's so sleazy, being secretive. I just don't see—'

'Just trust me, Alice. I understand.'

'Oh, do you? And how I feel about Rudi?'

'Oh yes, dear. Indeed I do.'

'It's so fierce. So overwhelming.' Alice put her arms around her mother in an excess of emotion, holding tightly onto her.

'I know, sweetheart. I know,' Cynthia

soothed her.

'Is this the way you felt about Daddy?'

'Yes,' Cynthia remembered. Once, long ago what she felt had been as powerful as what her daughter was now feeling. Once. Long, long ago in the dim and distant past. She hoped this Rudolph Wolfe would not be at all like Victor. She prayed fiercely that he would be a nice man. It was so important. The most important thing in the world to Cynthia was to ease her daughter out into the world, the healthy world, to break the tight control Victor had on the girl and see to it that Alice found her feet so that she could acquire the confidence and courage to live her own life independently. Cynthia was very afraid that Victor would break the girl's spirit, cow her into rejecting suitors to keep his hold on her. Yet she also believed that Alice was enough her father's daughter not to allow herself to be pushed around. She would accept reasonable control, but would, her mother believed, balk at excess.

At the moment Cynthia's main task, her prime concern, was to keep her husband in ignorance of Alice's girlish passion and as far as possible avert trouble.

She hugged her child and admitted that yes, it was how she'd once felt for Victor Sandar. The thought made her sad. How could she ever have been starry-eyed about that monster? It was a horrible thing to have to face; that that first sweet overwhelming passion usually metamorphosized into friendship, affection, toleration, indifference, or hatred. Which of these inevitable endings waited to overtake her beloved daughter? Only time would tell. But, Cynthia acknowledged sadly, passion always died.

'You'll help me, Mummy?' Alice asked anxiously.

'Of course, my darling,' Cynthia replied firmly. 'You can rely on that. I most certainly will help you.'

Alice, her mother was determined, would escape from the Sandar prison and lead a normal life. Cynthia often wondered if she would have stayed with Victor if she did not have Alice to tie her to her husband. She was not at all sure. She hoped she would have run away, escaped from bondage, but she decided it might have taken more courage than she believed herself capable of. So how much more difficult it would be for Alice, his daughter, who thought he was some kind of hero? Who remained in ignorance of his true nature? Cynthia knew that if she had left him he would never have rested until she had been eliminated. He would have sent men after her to execute her, she knew that. Victor was not as bad as he was painted, he was worse. But for all these years she had tried not to believe the worst. She had shied away from facing the fact that he could be capable of some of the things he was accused of.

She pushed her daughter's hair back from her forehead and looked into the huge troubled eyes. She leaned forward and kissed Alice's brow. 'What else is a mother for?' she asked, smiling, projecting a confidence she did not feel.

*     *     *

Martin had spent his day prowling around the Sandar villa. It was easy to find. Everyone knew where the notorious Victor Sandar lived and were only too happy to point it out.

'*Monsieur Sandar . . . oui monsieur, Villa Bella Vista. C'est là . . .*'

It was, he discovered, beside the *Villa Beau Rivage*. It was heavily guarded. Well, he expected that. All the beautiful homes on the Cap had tight security, they'd be daft if they didn't, but that, Martin knew, did not mean they were impenetrable. There was always a way in.

He'd talked to Jean-Marc Lelouche who was the gardener at the Sandar villa. He hung out in the local *Bar/Tabac,* was monosyllabic, uncommunicative and obviously disliked his boss. But he did like his wine. One evening in his cups he let slip a very interesting fact. Apparently the other night a young fellow had climbed up a tree in the Villa next door to the Sandars' and had had a talk with the Big Man's daughter. Jean-Marc laughed, wiping his copious moustache with the back of his hand. 'Mr Sandar, he did not know, he would have gone crazy if he had found out, but who would tell him? Who would dare? And it would serve the bastard right if his daughter out of whose arse he think the sun shine ran off with some layabout.' He made a suggestion, obviously ribald that Martin did not understand though he guessed the implication.

At first Martin was surprised that the gardener spoke any English at all, but the man explained that you had to speak English to be in Sandar's employ. 'He has no French, this man, so powerful, living here, he does not bother to learn the language,' the Frenchman sputtered, then continued ruminatively, 'His daughter is guarded night and day, like in a fortress, with the alarms, the video cameras, the dogs, the guards. But this Romeo, he climbs a tree next door, he talks to the princess in her boudoir.' He shrugged. 'No sirens, no dogs, no camera.' The gardener shook his head. 'Nothing. *Voila!* Can you believe it?' He stared in disbelief at Martin, amazed at the ridiculous folly of the human race.

Martin explored. He found the Crawley villa, which was not nearly so security-conscious, and scouted around. But people stared at him, noted his presence and he realised that he looked out of place. The last thing he wanted to do was stick out from the crowd and reluctantly he became aware that he looked ludicrous in his dark English suit wandering up and down the Boulevard du Cap in his warm clothes. He was canny enough to realise that people found him noticeable and it was vital that he blended.

So he bought himself a pair of white deck pants and a couple of tee shirts, and a tube of fake tan which he applied in the little room, not very expertly.

He decided to somehow get himself into that tree that overlooked the Sandar villa. If he was caught he could pretend he was interested in the Crawleys, not Victor Sandar, and not having taken anything they could not hold him. He was not a burglar. He'd make an excuse, say that he'd lost his way, climbed fences until he found himself in the Crawleys' garden. It did not matter whether they believed him or not. They couldn't hold him when all he'd done was trespass on the Crawleys' property.

He'd throw the gun away if they found him before he'd used it. It would mean he'd have to get another and that would be a nuisance, but Martin had patience. He was in no hurry. He wanted to get this right. As long as his mother was in hospital he had the time.

He called her every day. God bless the National Health Service. His mother had a phone beside her bed and could talk to him any time at all. She thought he was having a holiday. She thought he was still in England.

He said he'd nipped down to Bournemouth for a few days. He did not want to cause her any more anxiety.

It was difficult to conceal the gun wearing the new clothes. There seemed nowhere he could hide it. Then, observing the flow of tourists passing him by as he drank his *café au lait* in the *Bar/Tabac* he'd got into the habit of frequenting, he noticed that a lot of the men wore money belts around their waists. So he bought a large one and found to his relief that the gun fitted snugly into it. Now, he, Martin Sloane, looked like a hundred other of the less affluent tourists on the Côte d'Azur. He could go about his task, unnoticed, unremarkable, but eventually lethal.

## CHAPTER TWELVE

The Princess's party was being given for her by Buck Barrington the Third. The Princess was penniless but of impeccable lineage and Buck Barrington the Third liked to be able to list the names of the high and mighty he consorted and was photographed with in Europe to an attentive audience over his dinner table in Dallas, Texas. Buck Barrington the Third also had a great deal of money.

The cast list for the party included anyone who was anyone on the Côte d'Azur and a lot of wannabes as well. Buck Barrington the Third couldn't really tell the difference, but that did not matter—neither could his friends at home.

It was a glittering gathering. The women wore dresses by Yves St Laurent, Valentino and Versace, although the Princess herself wore a little number run up for her by an aged *vendeuse* in Juan les Pins. The guests were decked in sumptuous jewellery by Cartier and Bulgari though the Princess was decked out in paste. All her jewellery had gone long ago to pay her bills.

The Crawley party, back from Sardinia a couple of shades darker, were there at the invitation of Cynthia. She had told them to bring Jonathan and his young friends, especially Rudolph Wolfe who seemed so popular.

'You know, my dear, how boring these parties can be when everyone there is over fifty.'

'But Mrs Sandar, you and I are not—'

'No, no. You know what I mean. Old fogies.'

'Brompton and I are certainly not—'

'Alice is coming with me and I'd like her to meet some young people.'

'So Mr Sandar is not—'

'No. He'll not be joining us. Pressure of work, I'm afraid.' And the click of the telephone being replaced.

'What was she *really* saying?' Angelica

Crawley mused. Brompton Crawley shook his head. The social mores were not, as he often said, his bag.

'I think she wants Alice to meet Rudolph Wolfe. I wonder why?'

Brompton took a tug on his cigar. 'It's better than having her eye on Jonathan. I'd hate him to get mixed up with that crook. Dangerous.'

A soft look flooded Angelica's face. 'Jonathan is too sensible, Brompton.' She smiled fondly at the thought of her son, then frowned. 'Victor is not going to be there. What game is Cynthia playing? And she's never invited us to be in her party before. I wonder what she's manoeuvring.'

'Dangerous, I'll be bound. Anything to do with Sandar is dangerous.'

'Still, I'm delighted she asked us to join their party. It will do us no harm down here, to be seen with Lady Cynthia.'

She had some trouble persuading her son, who had changed his mind about wanting to go.

'Oh Ma, it's so uncool! And it's not Rudi's thing at all.'

'You get him there if you have to drag him,' Angelica ordered her son. 'I don't often ask you to do anything for me but please, please do this.'

Jonathan looked sulky. 'It's naff!' he muttered.

'*Jonathan!*'

'Oh all right then. But don't blame me if Rudi digs his heels in.'

His mother adopted her Medusa look. 'Get him there if you have to drag him by the hair. You hear me?'

To Jonathan's surprise Rudi readily agreed to join the party at the *Hôtel de Paris* and though Jonathan grimaced violently and wriggled uncomfortably at the mere thought, all his friend could say was, 'If Mrs Sandar has asked us, then we must go.'

When they arrived the orchestra was playing Cole Porter, Gershwin and romantic songs from musicals. Jonathan was disgusted. 'Typical oldies' bash,' he moaned to his mother and Amber in her green evening dress as he surveyed the chandelier-lit room. Small candlelit tables dotted the periphery of the dance floor and were tucked into alcoves. On the dance floor itself crowds of swirling couples twirled, executing foxtrots, waltzes, quick-steps and tangos. At the moment they were bounding about to a sparkling rendition of 'Do, do, do what you done, done before, baby'.

'Gross,' Amber groaned.

'Gross,' Jonathan muttered through his teeth and sighed and resigned himself to a painfully boring evening.

'You don't like it, Jonathan, because you can't dance,' Cynthia announced. 'Not proper dancing that is. Oh, you can gyrate about to pop in your own space but you're quite incapable of leading a partner and you're intimidated by the sight of the smoothly professional two-stepping and waltzing your elders are so proficient at.'

'Why'd we have to come?' Jonathan moaned. The only reason he'd made the effort—that is, apart from his mother's command and her threat to cut off his allowance—was to spend some time with Rudi, but from the start this proved impossible. Rudi Wolfe was otherwise engaged and Jonathan was fed up.

'Bloody boring! Bloody, bloody boring,' he muttered belligerently.

Angelica was resplendent in a clinging gold lamé gown split to the hip. She was not, however, at ease with herself in the creation. What was she revealing? How much crotch could they see? Was it cool? Did she look ridiculous? The questions swirled around in her brain giving her no peace. She could well do without her son's complaining.

She glanced at him, acutely irritated. 'Jonathan, you're the uncool one! We were invited, I don't know how or why. Cynthia Sandar has never been so friendly before and we're lucky to be here. All the best people are. So shut up and behave or I'll cut your allowance *right off*. Got that? I've always wanted to meet the Princess and get in with that set, and for some extraordinary reason Cynthia wants you and Rudi here so down, boy, down or I'll kill you.'

Angelica was not given to idle promises and the thought of his allowance being cut quite off made Jonathan feel wobbly. It quelled any rebellion in the young man. He lapsed into instant obedience.

They waited in line to be received. The Princess greeted them graciously. To Angelica's delight she seemed to know who they were and appeared to be delighted to see them, although she was vague about accepting Angelica's invitation to dinner the next week.

'A little gathering of dear familiar friends, you know.' She was a charming old dear, Angelica thought, if a bit vague.

To tell the truth, the Princess was not at all sure that she wanted to be here, the guest of honour at this ostentatious gathering. She enjoyed small dinner parties at the villas of her cronies but being on display was not really to her taste. However, she was very poor and the Barringtons were paying handsomely for her presence there. In fact, she need not worry about her bills and debts for the next year at least which was a very comforting thought and every time it crossed her mind that she'd rather be elsewhere she remembered the money, brightened up considerably and greeted the next guest with uncharacteristic enthusiasm.

112

Angelica saw that Cynthia was waving to them, beckoning them over, indicating a table she must have reserved for them. Angelica was faintly surprised at her eagerness. Cynthia was not an eager person and had never shown any desire to be friendly with her neighbours. In fact, quite the opposite—if anything, she had repulsed the Crawley's overtures. However, Angelica decided not to trouble herself with the whys and wherefores. She seized the opportunity to climb the social ladder with determination and verve.

To Angelica's delight Nola Reine was a member of the group. The slightly vulgar streak in the Comtesse gave Angelica confidence and the party settled down together and got on with the business of enjoying themselves.

Waiters moved swiftly here and there with trays of champagne and, sipping hers, Cynthia saw Rudi Wolfe enter the room. She knew who he was before Jonathan leapt from his seat and hailed the newcomer, for Nola Reine cried, 'Ah look! There's Rudi Wolfe. What a beautiful and charming young man he is.' Her eyes sparkled and Cynthia, gazing towards the entrance, could not but agree.

He stood at the top of the short flight of steps that led into the ballroom, staring at Alice who sat beside her mother. He was tall and handsome, it was true, but Cynthia noted he had an air about him of strength, an aura of sadness that set him apart, something indefinable that suggested self-sufficiency; a man in charge of himself. He just might, just might be a match for Victor Sandar. It surprised her, this strength he exuded; this unselfconscious self-containment seemed strange in one the same age as Jonathan Crawley.

He crossed the room to them. The Crawleys greeted him gustily, then Cynthia was introduced and they shook hands. His eyes, meeting hers, were candid and confident.

Cynthia bowed slightly to the Comtesse. 'This is—' she began, but the young man bent and kissed the old lady's hand. 'How delightful to see you again,' he cried with obvious joy.

'And this is my daughter,' Cynthia said.

For a moment it seemed to everyone that everything went very still and then Nola laughed.

'Cynthia, see how he stares at Alice. Obviously those two have clicked.' She had felt that terrible twinge of jealousy that only an ageing beauty with whom every man fell in love could feel when she realised her day had passed for ever and no beautiful young man would ever desire her again. The remark was catty and she regretted it instantly but to her surprise Cynthia breathed, 'Oh, I hope so.'

Nola plucked Cynthia's dress and Alice's mother removed her gaze from the young man and looked down into the wrinkled face of the old lady. She was surprised by the concern she saw there.

'If that's the case, be careful my dear,' Nola whispered.

'How do you mean?' she asked.

'I mean Victor. Be very careful.'

A chill crept down Cynthia's body and she shivered. She wondered briefly how Nola Reine, the Comtesse de Sevigné, could predict what was sure to happen, but she set her mouth stubbornly and looked away to where Rudi was staring at her daughter.

Alice looked so beautiful to him that his breath seemed to catch in his throat and it was difficult to breathe. There was a pounding in his chest and he unconsciously put his hand there for it seemed his heart would leap like a salmon out of his body and fly to her. She sat beside her mother wearing the beaded dress. Little pearls and diamanté and milk-coloured spangles covered the flesh-coloured chiffon sheath in a complicated pattern and when she moved or breathed a million sparkling darts of rosy light clothed her in radiance. Her hair, spun gold, was piled around her head woven with sparkling clusters. Around her long pale neck she wore a collar of seed pearls, six strands that forced her to hold her head high and proud. The expression in her soft, brown-velvet eyes held such ardent yearning as she returned his gaze that it nearly unmanned him.

Their looks met and intermingled. He was

so tall, she thought, so handsome in his dark evening clothes. He did not wear a cream-coloured dinner jacket like the other men but a chic Nehru tunic with its high collar. It made him stand out from all the crowd, different and special.

She had spent her life so tranquilly up to now. No storms had shaken her quiet existence and there had been few emotional upheavals except for the times she heard her parents quarrel, which she thought was normal. These disagreements were short-lived—Victor did not permit long battles—in any event their disputes did not really disturb her peace. Protected by the convent from the usual storms and passions of youth, the pain of adolescence had mercifully passed her by, but conversely she had not been prepared at all for life. Now, at this moment, she was in hiatus, in emotional turmoil. Overwhelmed by a tidal wave of desire and love and ardour she felt as if she'd been jolted into quivering, pulsating life, kick-started on an emotional roller-coaster. She took a few steps towards the tall youth and ended in arms that had opened for her as if he were home.

They moved into the dance, the slow music washing over them, the bittersweet melody working its romantic magic, gazing at each other, oblivious of Cynthia staring at them. They danced to the slow waltz as if they had danced together a hundred times before, as if their bodies were familiar.

After that, close beside him, tucked in the protective circle of his arms, she moved with him, danced with him, sat with him, never a breath away, in a dream from which she did not want to wake. Unconscious of those around them, in a world of their own, they occupied a different place, saw things with different eyes.

'This is a situation,' Nola warned Cynthia.

'I know. But I'm glad,' Cynthia said. 'She needs to escape.'

'Be careful, my dear. You must be very careful.'

'Don't you think I know that?' Cynthia glared at the little woman. 'But what's the alternative? A prison sentence for my daughter?' She shook her head. 'No, no, no. No matter what the cost she must escape. Don't you see that?'

Nola nodded. 'I suppose!' she sighed. 'But I repeat, be careful.'

The music played. The party ate from a buffet: cold meats, crab and lobster, salmon in aspic. *Fraise du bois*, raspberries, crème fraiche. They drank champagne. But Rudi and Alice neither ate nor drank. They were rapt, in a spell, enchanted and bemused. Nothing, no one existed for them—only each other, the beloved other.

They hardly dared to touch, for each encounter of hand on hand, of cheek against cheek scorched them, set them on fire. Their thoughts were communicated silently as they gazed at each other, dazzled by the exchanged glances.

She felt an excitement that she'd never felt before, a breathstopping hectic thrill that she could not contain, that spilled over into her eyes.

'Oh, my darling.' It was the first thing he'd said to her that evening, though they'd been together all night. They had spoken to each other without speech. They danced and he whispered the endearment. He could feel the tickle of the tendrils of her soft hair near his ear, against his cheek and the sweetness of her breath as she sharply drew it in at his words. He felt weak and she leaned closer to him as if their bodies were one. She smiled up at him. The trust in her expression overwhelmed him. He felt empowered, as if he could fight dragons, climb mountains, achieve any damn thing he set his mind to when she looked at him like that.

She in her turn knew now that fairy tales were true. You did meet a handsome prince; if not exactly a Prince then certainly a prince among men. And she knew, just knew she'd rest here in his arms forever and live happily ever after.

'Oh my dearest one!'

'My darling Rudi.'

'I love you.'

'I love you.'

'From the first moment.'

'The first second!'

They did not speak these words, their eyes spoke them.

'Here is my heart,' hers said.

'And here is mine,' his returned.

The kiss he gave her was soft as the touch of a butterfly's wings yet startled and excited her as if it were as sharp as a bee sting. She'd never been kissed before and she felt, as in the fairy tales, that she had been awakened. She'd been sleepwalking all these years and now she'd been jolted into quivering life by a kiss, so tender, so sweet, so piercingly electric that it shot through her body like a fiery arrow.

'You've brought me to life. Breathed your love into me.' Again she did not say it but he understood. Her eyes told him, misty and yielding. They spoke volumes. No poetry he had ever read was as sweet. He touched the small of her back and his fingers burned. He held her, close yet carefully, as if she might break and she rested her forehead on his shoulder and the orchestra played *La Vie en Rose*.

'Rudi. Rudi,' she breathed aloud, a soft sigh making his name seem like music. He heard the whisper near his shoulder and he held her even closer, this precious, dearest being, his love, his life. They did not speak again for there was no need for words—'Soft eyes looked love to eyes that spake again.'

Cynthia watched through half-closed lids. She too was filled with emotion, watching the young couple on the dance floor. But Cynthia's emotions were of fear, panic, terror even. Her plan had worked far too well and it was too late now to halt it. There was no way to unpick the tapestry of this evening, change the events, put the clock back.

She had hoped for an attraction, a flirtation, a lighthearted tentative exploration, not this explosion of obvious blazing passion. What was she to do now? She tried to still a heart beating as hectically as her daughter's and asked herself, What would happen next? She cursed the fact that she had not listened to Nola de Sevigné. The old Comtesse had been right.

That Victor would not tolerate it went without saying. That he'd blame her, ditto. She had thought that Alice would enjoy a dalliance with the handsome Rudi and *herself* stand up to her father, find her feet and move on. Victor could never be angry with Alice for long and she, Cynthia, would not come into his line of fire.

But there would be hell to pay, the situation being as it was tonight. At the centre of the whole thing were her daughter's delicate feelings. It was obvious to anyone even remotely perceptive that Alice had passed a point of no return and was passionately—

madly, yes, that was it, madly—in love. Also it was patently obvious that this young man, this Rudi Wolfe, was not an emotionally confused, immature young man and this was not a dalliance. He was a force to be reckoned with, and Cynthia, try as she might, could see nothing ahead but tragedy.

But what could she do? No answer came readily to mind and all around her the cacophony of chatter and music, gossip and laughter, and the clink of cutlery rose and fell like the sound of the sea breaking on the shore. Only Nola Reine, when she caught the aged film star's eyes, seemed to comprehend the dangerous situation.

Victor would not permit this. There would be no quiet development, no tentative exploring and boys coming and going with Victor ordering them out of the house and Alice growing stronger, more determined. Alice had committed herself to this man and from complete unawakened innocence she had leapt to full-blown passionate love. There would be no development period, no gradual growth and what Victor would do when he found out caused Cynthia to shudder.

And Alice was not equipped to deal with her father. She would not understand why her Daddy wasn't pleased that she had found love. How to explain to her that the Daddy she loved and trusted was going to be outraged? How to avoid the inevitable disillusionment?

Alice was going to be hurt no matter what happened. Either her father or her lover would kill the innocent joy in those big brown eyes.

Cynthia wished it would not happen just yet. She wished with all her heart that her daughter could hold on to her belief that nothing bad could ever happen to her, that the world was a benign and kindly place, that her father and mother were perfect, like gods, and that her prince would marry her and they would live happily ever after.

Her reverie was interrupted. 'Mrs Sandar, it is so nice to see you here.' The Princess had come to the table without Cynthia noticing.

The Princess had been dancing with the young Comte d'Allenbert and he stood now behind her as she sat, a little breathless, beside the Englishwoman.

'I don't know half the people here yet they claim an intimate knowledge of me,' she told Cynthia confidingly, fanning herself with a tiny hand-painted fan she held. It was on a ribbon around her wrist, almost invisible under the soft rolls of her flesh. 'Ghastly! The Riviera has gone down, you know, since the twenties and thirties. Before Hitler. It's a playground now for the *hoi polloi*. All sorts of riff-raff about.' She glanced about the ballroom, shaking her tight little curls. 'All the gentlemen died in the last war, my dear,' she said. 'There are none around today.' Her plump cheeks were hotly red and she picked up Alice's untouched glass of champagne and downed it in one gulp.

'*Est-ce que je peux vous cherchez quelquechose?*' the young Comte dutifully offered. Then with a smile at Cynthia he added in English, 'I have promised to see the Princess back to her table.' A penniless noble, he acted as her walker in return for his supper, free drinks and a tolerable room in her villa.

'In a moment, Albert. In a moment. As I was saying, *cherie*, the place has lost its style. Its *élan*. Look, for instance, there.' She snapped the fan shut and pointed it where Buck Barrington the Third danced boisterously with his wife. 'Our host. What is he dressed up as? Please tell me that. I wish to know.'

Buck wore a tartan jacket in a light viscose and silk mix. His wife was decked out in an evening dress that, Angelica remarked, made her look like Nell Gwyn. 'All bust, no brain.'

'Oh, I don't know,' Cynthia said. 'He dances well,' she told the Princess, who wasn't listening.

'And that young man there. Couldn't help noticing him. He's so completely out of place. And no one seems to know him.' She snapped her fan shut and pointed—quite rudely, Cynthia thought, although the French had different views to the English about that. She was indicating a young man with a bony face and an anguished expression who was lounging against a pillar, looking awkward. He seemed to be scanning the crowd as if searching for someone he knew. His evening clothes, like Rudi's, were dark but unlike Rudi's they were abominably cut, obviously cheap and hung about his person scarecrow-fashion. Cynthia decided he probably came from an impoverished noble family, then discarded the idea. The clothes belied this; she'd never known a wellbred family to buy cheap. They all managed at least one decent evening suit, even if it was worn to a thread, even if it was papa's hand-me-down. Or even grandpapa's.

And what on earth was he doing at a ball with a money-belt around his waist? Heavens, the Princess was right. Things had come to a pretty pass!

As Cynthia watched, the young man caught her eye and to her surprise he hurried away towards the exit. She wanted to rush after him and say, 'I won't hurt you,' but she simply watched him go.

'I'm always nervous of cutting someone like him,' the Princess was saying. 'Perhaps offending some poor king or other whose son or nephew he is. Hurting an old friend fallen on hard times.' The Princess echoed Cynthia's thoughts, 'Still, it is a bit much! Clothes fit only for salesmen. *Mon Dieu,* what is the world coming to?' She shook her fan open again with a deft flick of her wrist and fanned herself for a while, then snapped it shut again. She raised it and indicated Rudi and Alice who moved together slowly, gracefully to the swelling violins and clarinet playing 'Smoke Gets in Your Eyes'.

'Now there!' she cried. '*That's* style. That's elegance. That's how it should be.' She sighed theatrically. '*L'amour!* Oh, *Mon Dieu*, how sad to be old! Past it! Look at them. Like poetry. So beautiful. So *triste!*'

'Why do you say that?' Cynthia asked sharply, somewhat paranoid.

The Princess shrugged. 'Because it will not last. It will vanish. Love always does. Phut! Like a candle, guttering out.' She shook her head. Then she brightened. 'Perhaps it is better not to mourn love's passing. Not to be sad that one is no longer young. Perhaps after all it is better to be past all that pain, no? You and I, Cynthia, will not be so alive, so . . .' She searched for a moment, then continued. 'So *desperate,* so acutely vulnerable and at the mercy of fate again, and perhaps that is a good thing. Young love, after all, is agony!' And she rose, kissed Cynthia on both cheeks and, tapping the young Comte on his shoulder with her fan, moved away from them.

Cynthia stared after her. No one knew, least of all the Princess, the time bomb that was going to explode when the beautiful young couple, envied she realised by most of the crowd present, were discovered by the girl's

125

father.

Angelica was surprised when, returning to the table after a nostalgic dance with Brompton, she saw that Cynthia's eyes were full of tears. 'Oh my dear, what's the matter?' she asked. Cynthia took a tissue from her evening purse and gently dabbed her eyes.

'Nothing, really.' She smiled at Angelica, 'It's just . . .' She shrugged. 'Oh, why do children have to grow up?' she asked wistfully.

\*          \*          \*

He was intelligent—probably intellectual. Alice gazed at him, bemused, enchanted, her body melting in his arms. She knew she was ignorant, acutely aware of how naïve she must seem to him, he who was so sophisticated. A real man. Like her father. Mature and self-contained. How could he care for someone as stupidly gauche as she? She'd soon bore him. He'd quickly tire of her. She gazed up at him, anxiety clouding her eyes.

'I'm not . . .' She stumbled to a halt. 'I'm not clever,' she said.

He threw back his head and laughed. It was the first time he'd really laughed since he'd left the war zone.

'What's that got to do with anything?' he enquired, head cocked to one side, loving her naïveté.

'I'll soon bore you,' she said, making a face.

126

'Honey, you stop this right now,' he ordered. 'Clever is the last thing I want. *You* are what I want.'

She gulped. He'd said it. He wanted her. But still she quibbled, 'You've been out there, in the world, earning your living, while I've been shut away in a *convent* in *Spain*! *Granada!* Not even Madrid!'

He laughed again. 'So much the better. You're not yet tainted by cynicism, by the frantic ambition that drives people, the money-grabbing, the rush for success, the jockeying for position and power, for recognition—for a mention in *Hello!* magazine, for God's sake. That terrible rush that drives people crazy out there in the big wide world.' He smiled down at her, reassuring her. 'For that I am profoundly grateful, my love.'

She cocked her head, contemplating his face, familiarising herself with its planes, its beautiful features, the strength and tenderness inherent in the warmth of his smile, the melancholy in his eyes.

'What do you do out there in the big wide world?' she asked shyly and his heart skipped a beat. 'I know so little about you,' she continued. 'Not that it matters,' she added hastily.

'We have the rest of our lives to discover each other,' he said, then added, 'I'm a writer. I've just come back from the war in Yugoslavia.'

'That explains it.'

'What?' he asked, a little apprehensively.

'The sadness in your eyes,' she said and touched his temple tenderly with her fingers. 'Dearest, dearest man. I promise to take it away,' she whispered.

She would wipe the sadness from his eyes and make them drowsy with love for her. She would make him forget pain and suffering, tragedy and grief. She would transform his life and help him to be joyous again, to forget the pain of the society man had created, the society he deplored so much. She would make him see the beauty of God's world, of nature. Of her.

## CHAPTER THIRTEEN

'The little scrote is gorn.' The voice was close, as if Eddie was in the room with him.

'Can't be!' Victor's brain went swiftly into first gear, working it out, what it meant.

'Is! What d'you want us to do? Deal with the rest of the harvest? Take care of it?'

He meant Mrs Sloane. Their phones were bugged, Victor knew that, so they spoke in code, in case anyone was listening. Victor laughed harshly. Anyone listening would think he was a bloody farmer. They talked of the price of grain. Harvests. Vineyards yield, and such like.

At this news Victor ground his back teeth. His dentist said the erosion was appalling.

Why hadn't he dealt with that woman and her son long ago? He was too soft by half. He knew why though. The code, much stricter then. It was a stern code, an inflexible one. East Enders didn't rub out women and children. Didn't hurt them, rather protected them. It was not on. To do so would ruin his reputation, cast a slur. He was the hard man, the top man, but he was not a bully. Didn't pick on women or kids.

He wished it wasn't so. As long as that cow lived there was danger for him. She was an aggravation he could well do without, Mrs Sloane was. And now Eddie was telling him the son had flown the coop.

Victor was shocked when he realised that the son would be grown up by now. He'd always thought of Martin Sloane as a child. But time passed. He was getting old. It was not a pleasant thought. He thought of Cynthia, her hoity-toity airs. He remembered Alison Linten, little Allie, all curves and sauce and big bosoms and smart cracks; cheeky repartee. Tossing her head. Provocative! She gave off a heat that reeked of sex and excited him even now when he thought of her. The wiggle when she walked. The puff of bleached hair that turned him on. Why hadn't he married Allie? He was so much more comfortable with her than with Cynthia. He was himself in her company. He could relax with Allie. Why had he chosen to saddle himself with an upper-class bitch who challenged him at every turn, made him feel inferior no matter how he tried to dominate her; *did* dominate her. But she was elusive and even when she did as he ordered she somehow, by her expression, her manner, was the victor. So why had he chosen her?

He'd been ambitious, that was why, he answered himself. He'd always run after the next unattainable thing, person, object, and had not been satisfied until he got it; had not been satisfied when he *had* got it, had hurried ever onwards and upwards to the next person, thing, object, the slope getting slippier all the time.

'You there, boss?' The voice sounded in his ear.

'Yeah, Eddie. No. Leave the harvest alone.'

'You sure?'

'I'm sure. But look for the reaper. Not too hard mind. He'll come home for the harvest. Bound to. Then deal. He's a man now, isn't he?'

'The full enchilada?'

'The full Monty.'

He replaced the receiver. It surprised him that the Sloane boy had disobeyed rules. He was a nonentity, a useless little runt of no threat whatsoever to Victor Sandar, so why worry? He probably simply wanted to get away from his mum, cut the apron strings, see some life. So he ran. Yes, that was it.

Well, he wasn't important. A little dispensible flea in the scheme of things, someone to stamp on, grind underfoot.

Victor lit a cigar. He turned his head as he heard the car draw to a halt on the gravel outside. He walked to the window.

A sickle moon hung in a black satin sky and there was a breathless hush over the evening. The stars were dancing and winking and the scent of jasmine was heavy in the air. Then below him the sound of voices carried on the balmy night. A car drew to a halt, scrunching on the gravel.

As he watched he saw Cynthia alighting from the Mercedes. She was saying something to Alice as his daughter climbed out of the car; sliding carefully because her shimmering dress was so slim-fitting, she slipped like a silver fish out onto the drive. He leaned forward for his wife's voice held a note of panic that was unusual for her.

'—you can't, Alice. Your father will not like it at all.' Her voice carried clearly up to him and he could hear over it Alice's protests.

'Nonsense, Mummy. I want Daddy to meet Rudi. He'll be delighted, you'll see.'

His heart, as always, rose at the sight of his lovely child but then thudded cruelly at her words. Meet who? Who was she talking about?

And in that moment he saw the young man unwind himself out of the car, a tall lean shape against the moon. He hurried around to Alice—he was a tall, handsome young man—and he stood, his arm around her possessively, smiling at her, a soft intimate smile which she returned.

Rage flooded Victor, almost blinding him. He stepped forward on the balcony, fury bubbling inside him like a volcano. He was yelling, 'Take your goddamned hands offa her,' when he was cut short and the shot rang out.

At first he thought the pain that seared him was the pain of his daughter's betrayal. How could she look that way at another man? Then he saw the shadows move, the layers of black on black coalesce and take the shape of a man. A shadowy figure who must have been concealed in the trees next door, a white moon-face peering through the leaves, a shocked expression on that face.

Victor tried to point at the man who was now leaping away. He tried to draw the watchers' attention to the intruder who was obviously escaping but he found he could not speak or move. He was sinking slowly to the ground. As if from far away he heard the sound of the alarms go off, scaring the daylights out of the wildlife, the birds winging wildly out of the trees and, like the intruder, vanishing on the darkening air. Then

132

everything swam blackly before his eyes. He saw as if in a dream his wife's bewildered face, heard his daughter cry out, 'Daddy! Daddy!' Then the pain took over, swamping him in excruciating agony, and he thought, So this is what it's like. Pain. Oh, Jesus H. Christ, I never knew it was like this. The agony. The excruciating agony. And the even more terrible truth seared his brain. My Alice is in love with that man. Oh God, she thinks she loves him. Well, that has to be stopped. And then the agony bore him away to a place out of the reach of any one of them, into oblivion.

## CHAPTER FOURTEEN

When Martin shinned down the tree, skirting the lawn in the shadows, his heart was pounding against his chest and there was a fearful roaring in his ears.

He'd done it! He'd pulled the trigger and seen his mortal enemy fall. He felt like whooping aloud, punching his fists in the air, crying out to the world in triumph. But under the triumph there was a hollow emptiness.

He had to be quiet as a mouse, creeping out of the Crawley compound, silently, surreptitiously.

So it was with considerable alarm that, keeping closely to the dividing hedge, trampling through the border plants, he nearly tripped over someone sitting there, almost completely concealed by the foliage.

The person, to his consternation, yelled out, 'What the hell—' and Martin clapped his hand over her mouth, for he realised the solitary stranger sitting cross-legged on the ground was a girl.

The encounter, so unexpected, threw him off-balance. Who was she? A servant? One of the Crawleys? An interloper like himself? Someone who would recognise him instantly as an intruder? She was struggling like a landed fish as he tried to hold onto her and at the same time keep her quiet.

'Will you be quiet if I take my hand away?' he hissed in her ear. He knew he could not hold onto her for long; he was shaking too much and the only thing that prevented her from knocking him over and running away was her surprise.

She nodded fearfully and he let her go.

'God, you smell,' she whispered, brushing herself down.

He reeked of fear. He realised he'd been sweating since he climbed the tree. No, probably since he left the room in the *pension*.

'Ouch! You're hurting,' she cried quietly as he gripped her wrists. He was grateful that she was so docile. He hated violence, did not want to be forced to hurt her. He smiled to himself at the irony. Here he was, worried about clutching a girl's wrists in a fierce grip when he'd just killed a man.

'Sorry,' he said.

They were seated side by side, whispering now.

'What are you doing here?' the girl asked. 'I thought I heard shots.'

'Shut up!' he hissed in panic. He wanted to extricate himself, wanted to escape. But he knew he couldn't just up and run away leaving her here to tell about his presence, describe him to the *gendarmes*.

They sat there concealed by the ferns, hidden in the bushes. There were people running across from the other side of the Crawley villa. They had not seemed to be there when he'd hidden in the trees in wait for Victor Sandar.

They'd have sent for the police by now. He was a goner if she chose to make a fuss. He stared down at her, his face twitching with anxiety. She was a tiny redhead and she smiled slyly at him. To his surprise she did not seem disposed to shout for help or create a disturbance.

His heart was pounding as she peered at him in the gloaming. She was wearing an emerald-green taffeta ballgown which was crushed and stained.

'You shot him, didn't you?' she whispered, her voice eager. He nodded. No use denying it. He was for the high jump.

135

The voices, the commotion of people speculating, gathering on both sides of the hedge was louder now. The redhead glanced at the gun he held in his right hand. His eyes followed her glance.

'Gimme that,' she ordered, prising the gun from his fierce grip. She shoved it into an evening bag encrusted with emerald-green spangles. 'Now kiss me!' she ordered. She pulled his arms around her waist and began to kiss him with startling thoroughness.

'Amber? That you?' a voice called. The girl pulled her face back and looked up at the people standing above her.

'Sure. What's up Jonathan?'

'God, you stoned or something? There were shots from the Sandar villa. Are you deaf? Hey, who's that with you?'

'I'm not listening Jonathan. Can't you see I'm busy? Bet you're wrong. Musta been a car backfiring.'

'No. There's police all over. Can't you hear the sirens? You must be deaf.'

'No. Just otherwise occupied!' Amber kissed Martin again.

'I think that must be the ambulance,' Jonathan cried. He pointed to Martin. 'Who the hell is he?'

'Amber!' It was a woman's voice. 'What *are* you doing? Who is this young man?'

'He's the flavour of the month, obviously,' Jonathan muttered dryly.

'He's a friend of my brother's, Mrs Crawley,' Amber proclaimed and holding Martin's hand she pulled him to his feet and dragged him away from the Sandar side of the villa, across the terrace and past the dining area.

'Where are you going?' Mrs Crawley cried after them as they ran.

'We're off to St Trop to get more action,' Amber cried.

'I would have thought there was quite enough action in the Sandar back yard,' Angelica said dryly.

As they ran Martin saw a man sitting on the terrace puffing on a cigar, paying no attention to anything. A couple of servants fussed about him pouring coffee.

'Ta-ra, Mr Crawley,' Amber shouted as they passed, then to Martin, 'He always drinks coffee late at night then wonders why he can't sleep. He's a famous insomniac.'

Martin was pulled along willy-nilly until they reached the driveway where the cars were parked.

'Come on! Get in,' she ordered and jumped into a Volkswagen, getting the key from her emerald bag. She shouted once more to Martin who reluctantly did as she commanded and, turning the key, she revved up the small automobile and drove wildly and erratically onto the Boulevard du Cap and down the hill towards Antibes.

On the way down she had to pull over to allow an ambulance, which was roaring up towards the villas, to pass by.

Martin held onto the strap above the window. She was not a good driver. Not that he cared. He had a sense of light-headedness and irresponsibility as if what had happened took place in a dream.

'I hope you didn't miss,' Amber said glancing in the mirror at the retreating ambulance. 'I hope you were lethal.' Her face was hard in the moonlight, fierce and angry. 'All I hope is you took him right out.'

'All *I* hope is I hit *him*. That there was no one else. That I didn't get someone else as well.'

'Gosh, wouldn't you *know*? If you're a contract killer you gotta be professional.' She glanced at him out of the corner of her eye while handling the car slightly more competently than before.

'I've never used a gun before in my life,' Martin protested, startled by her assumption. She looked at him incredulously as she pulled the car up in front of a red light.

'You're *not* a contract gunman?' she asked.

'No. I am not,' he reiterated firmly.

'But everyone knew there was a contract out on him,' she said.

'Well, maybe. But I'm not that.'

'Then who the hell are you?' she asked.

'I'll tell you when we . . . where are we

going?'

'St Tropez. I thought it best to do as I said we were going to. In case questions are asked afterwards. In case they check on our movements.'

She drove the car along the coast road. They had to crawl, for the crowds surged up and down and a crocodile of red rear lights circled the boulevard going one way, bright yellow the other, all at a snail's pace. The boutiques hummed, doing brisk business, and limousines pulled up to or were parked in the bays in front of glitzy, ritzy hotels buzzing with life. Amber tapped her fingers on the steering wheel as they crawled along. She was curiously silent. She steered the car down to where the big yachts were berthed in Golfe Juan and, parking the car, pulled him out after her.

'What are we—'

'C'mon.' She walked until she reached a fairly deserted spot. The water was black below them. On the yachts people moved behind Perspex as if in a dream. The sound of laughter echoed faintly across the water. Martin could see a man, tanned, silver-haired, in a white tuxedo, leaning on the rail of a huge yacht staring up at the moon. He wondered what the man could be thinking. He looked like an advertisement; perfect. The epitome of success. Yet the expression on his face lit by the moonlight was worried. Perhaps, Martin thought, he was a gambler. He could hear the swoosh-swoosh of the water at their feet.

Amber took the gun out of the bag, polished it thoroughly with a tissue, then dropped it into the black water and pulled him after her back to the car.

She turned to face him when they reached it.

'Why did you shoot him?' she asked.

'He murdered my father,' Martin told her. He was glad it was out now, glad he'd said it. Glad he could tell someone.

He thought she'd show surprise, some astonishment but she just nodded.

'Me too,' she said. 'And he might as well have murdered my mother.' This time it was Martin who nodded. Since her stroke his mother had been frail, so frail. That lay directly at Victor Sandar's door. The fear his mother lived with. The visits from Eddie the Ferret. The stroke and her subsequent fragility.

'He got all my father's money, tricked him out of it. Ruined him,' the girl, Amber, was saying. 'So my father shot himself. Then my mother had a nervous breakdown.'

'He does that,' Martin said. 'Destroys people.' The moonlight bathed her face in silver and she looked like a waif, a gypsy straggler in her green taffeta ballgown which was by now in a sorry state. Her hair fell about her face all tangled and her lip trembled.

'I thought you were a contract killer,' she

told him, jingling the car keys around her finger nervously.

'I don't even know what that is, exactly,' he replied uncertainly.

'You know! Someone paid a huge sum to knock people off. Usually in a power struggle. Like, someone wants to take over Victor Sandar's empire.'

'Well, that's not me,' he stammered, not knowing whether to be outraged or flattered. 'I'm not getting paid. There's no money involved.'

'Then why did you shoot him?' she asked.

'Because, like you, he destroyed my family.'

'What's your name?' she asked.

'Martin Sloane.'

She'd been watching the crowd above them passing by and now she turned her head and looked at him.

'Of course! I know you,' she exclaimed. 'All about you. Your father and Victor Sandar. I read all about it. I keep a check on him. I've read everything about him and his filthy career.' She smiled at him, 'I see!' she said as if everything had been satisfactorily explained. 'Get in. Let's go and have some coffee.'

They found a café and sat at a table on the sidewalk. She ordered the coffee. She was silent for a while, then she leaned across the table.

'Now listen to me,' she said. 'You were with me all evening. I saw you at the ball, Martin, so

141

I'll swear that you were my date. No one will argue. No one noticed. They were all too busy admiring Rudi and Alice Sandar.' She screwed up her face. 'You must say you're a friend of my brother Roger. He'll back up what I say when he knows the facts. He's been toying with the idea of taking Victor Sandar out himself. Just like me.'

'You wanted to kill him too?' Martin asked. She shrugged.

'Who doesn't?' she said. Then she frowned, thinking. He drank some more of the coffee, watching her.

'We're an item, you and me.'

'A what?'

'An *item*! We're having an affair, dummy,' she continued tranquilly. 'I asked you to meet me at the ball. We slipped away together because we were bored,'—she bit her lip—'and we wanted to snog.' She glanced at him, then raised an eyebrow. 'You know what that means, don't you?'

He nodded. 'Course I do.'

'We've been together ever since,' she finished happily.

'Didn't anyone see you? Could they say you were lying?'

She shook her head. 'No,' she replied tartly. 'I did slip away. I had something to, um . . . do. Get. I was elsewhere and those guys won't want to come forward to contradict my story. No way.' Her eyes narrowed and she grinned suddenly at him. 'No. You're safe with me,' she said. 'Where are you staying?' He told her and she laughed. 'How gross! Never mind. We can go there now. Stay awhile.'

'It's very late,' he said and she gave him a smirk.

'Don't worry. I'm not going to attack you, ravage you.' She laughed.

He didn't know quite what to do or say. He was an innocent in this context. He had only planned up to the shooting, no further, yet here he was in a whole different scenario, totally out of his depth.

However, she took charge. She was incisive and sure of herself. He was confused and bewildered. Had he really killed Victor Sandar? He ought to feel something but at the moment he didn't. He only felt curiously indifferent and tired. As if he'd been walking for miles and had stopped, the exhaustion finally hitting him. He'd planned this, dreamed of it for so long and now he felt empty and worn out. As if there was no purpose in his life any more.

He let her take charge, boss him around. He obeyed her because he could not think of anything else to do.

She paid for the coffee and they left. She drove back to his room and she followed him into the *pension*.

He fell on the bed in his clothes and went to sleep almost at once. He heard her say something like, 'What a dump!' and then he heard no more. He turned his head and his last fading memory was a hazy vision of her at the table in his room sniffing a white powder greedily as if her life depended on it.

## CHAPTER FIFTEEN

She'd pressed him to come inside for a nightcap and to meet her Daddy. Nothing Cynthia or Rudi could say dissuaded her. She was determined, certain her Daddy would be delighted for her, would naturally love her prince, her knight in shining armour. Why wouldn't he?

They did not see who shot Victor as he stood on the balcony silhouetted against the glow of lamplight behind him. They could see he was trying to say something, shout something. But they were so stunned when they heard the shot and he collapsed that not one of them moved for seconds. Moments. They did not look behind them. They were too surprised. Then Rudi shouted, 'Get an ambulance!' and Alice began moaning, 'Oh God, Oh God, Daddy!'

They all hurried inside, galvanised out of their shocked condition into action.

'I'll call the ambulance,' Cynthia cried and, to Rudi, 'You'd better go.'

'No,' Rudi answered, quietly, stubbornly. 'She needs me now.' He too went into the living-room.

Alice had rushed upstairs to get to the balcony and her father while Cynthia picked up the phone and dialled. Rudi stood uncertainly trying to get his bearings.

Cynthia, to her horror, was thinking how convenient it would be, how poetically just if Victor died now or was already dead, but Alice, leaning over the balustrade, just as she had that night when she'd heard them quarrelling, called out, 'He's alive! Oh hurry, Mummy, hurry.' Her lovely dress was covered in blood and she shouted down to her mother, 'He's alive! He's breathing. Get an ambulance quickly. Oh hurry, hurry.' She disappeared again and Rudi took the stairs two at a time after her. Cynthia reluctantly gave the address.

The ambulance arrived soon after the police. The air was filled with the shrill noises of sirens and alarms, the blue and red lights bouncing around over eucalyptus and hydrangea, casting a lurid glow over the more subtle shades of nature.

An oxygen mask was placed over Victor's nose and mouth and he was strapped to a gurney and put into the ambulance. It roared down the driveway bearing Cynthia and her husband to the hospital in Nice.

Alice answered the questions the *gendarmes* fired at her. No, she had not seen the gunman.

No, she could not describe him. How could she when she had not seen him? He must have been part of the shadows, there when they arrived home, but no, she could not help them with his identity. She knew of no reason why anyone would have wanted to kill her darling Daddy. She noticed the strange looks the uniformed police exchanged with the detectives as she talked about her father but she was too distracted to comment or pay much attention to their reaction.

'*Mon Dieu, je ne comprends pas*,' the young *gendarme* muttered but the detective shook his head at him reprovingly. Alice was not listening.

'When can I go to the hospital?' she asked the detective who seemed to be in charge.

'Whenever you like, mademoiselle. There is nothing more you can help us with.'

'You'll catch him?' she asked angrily. 'You don't seem to be making too much of an effort.' Again that exchange of glances.

'We will try, mademoiselle, but it will be difficult.' The *gendarmes* shrugged.

'Aren't you going to look for fingerprints? See if anyone next door saw him? Could identify him?' Her voice bordered on the hysterical.

'He was wearing gloves, this assassin, probably something over his head.' The detective made a face. 'There are a lot of people who want him dead. There'll be a lot of

146

suspects.'

'What on earth do you mean by that?' Alice sounded furious.

'If you do not know, mademoiselle, it is not my place to enlighten you.' The detective's voice was acid.

'Well, my father was an important man—'

'Notorious, I'd say,' the detective muttered.

'And you'd better find his murderer.'

'He's not dead, is he?'

'No, but—'

'Look, mademoiselle, we'll do our best.' He didn't sound too hopeful and Rudi, watching the police, got the distinct impression that they were not too bothered. Someone had tried to take out a gangster who lived, much against their will, on their patch. He got what he deserved. It was no outrage, it was almost inevitable so there was no urgency to find the killer, punish him.

'*Bonne chance . . .*' he heard one of the young *gendarmes* say to the other.

'We will do our best,' the detective was saying in placating tones to Alice.

'Come on, Rudi, let's go.'

He looked into her face, saw the shock and horror there and his heart swelled with pity. He wanted so badly to protect her, to guard her from the inevitable gossip and speculation, her realisation of how the world saw her father, for he had understood early on that she had absolutely no idea of the truth.

147

It probably would not be possible any longer to save her from the horror she would feel when the truth dawned. Her enlightenment would cost her dear. Now that this attempt had been made on her father's life she was bound to discover the truth about Victor Sandar and he knew that when she did he must be there to support her.

Of course she would not believe it. At first she would imagine everyone was lying, that a terrible mistake had been made. Then she would think it was jealousy. But little by little the painful facts would emerge, irrefutable facts. She'd be shocked and that lovely innocence would vanish forever. Acceptance of betrayal would become a necessity if she did not want to grow hard and bitter. His lovely, sweet angel was going to change dramatically.

At the hospital they waited. The doctors were not optimistic. They shook their heads and said Monsieur Sandar might not make it.

Alice, Cynthia and Rudi sat mostly in silence. There was a television screen above them in the cold green room. The sound was turned off. It was a sports channel, a peculiar choice for a hospital, Rudi thought. The racing drivers, the footballers and tennis champions talked and laughed animatedly in silence on the flickering screen. The room, which was more of an alcove, had no door and Alice paced the corridor, up and down, up and down. Rudi was never far away, watching her intently, waiting. Cynthia sat stony-faced, turning the pages of a magazine, lost in her own thoughts. Occasionally she stretched out and clasped her daughter's hand, then let it drop and returned to her ruminating.

'Who would want to kill Daddy? The detective said. . .'

'Don't think about it now,' Cynthia replied.

Alice looked at Rudi and her mother, a bewildered expression on her face. 'You've always said, Mummy, that there was a contract out on his life. What contract? Tell me now. I want to know.'

'It was nothing, sweetheart. Just . . .'

'What? Just what? I mean to find out, Mummy. I have to know. Before it was not important to me, but now—'

'There are some nasty people in London who want your father dead,' Cynthia said, her lips tight. She looked around wildly as if she wanted to escape. Why doesn't she tell her the truth? Rudi wondered. Why had they lied for so long? Then he realised that they probably had no choice. You can hardly tell a sweet innocent child that her father is a sadist and a killer.

'But why? Daddy's been out of London years and years. What could be so bad? What could he have done that someone would want to *kill* him?' Her face was a mask of anxiety. Cynthia closed the magazine and looked at her daughter. Her face changed and hardened.

She stared at Alice, then said coldly, firmly, 'One of the relations of the people *he* killed is my guess.'

Rudi drew in his breath. Why did she do it so suddenly?

Cynthia continued, 'I'm unable to tolerate the lie I've lived all these years. Your adoration of your father, sweetheart, sickens me.'

Alice gave a little moan. 'Oh, it's not true. Say it's not true. Mother, you're lying.'

In her anguish she turned to Rudi. He held her close for a moment. And for a moment there was silence, and the footballer overhead waved his arms about.

Cynthia was weeping. Alice had lost all her colour. She had exuded energy, a sort of radiant zest for life, a joy of living that communicated itself to all about her. But now, as he watched, Rudi saw all that energy evaporate like damp in the hot sun. She became lifeless before his eyes, a shell. A husk. Empty.

Cynthia pulled the girl towards her and like a rag doll Alice let herself be embraced. Limp and listless, she seemed in shock in her mother's arms.

'Oh my darling, I'm sorry. So sorry. But you had to know. You'd have found out any day now. The papers will be upon us relentlessly now this has happened. You're not at school any more, protected from the gossips, the

150

malicious . . .'

She talked on and on in soothing tones and Alice sat beside her mother in the circle of her arms like a dead thing.

They remained in the alcove off the main hospital corridor. White-coated men and women with stethoscope passed by every now and then, not giving them a glance, their concentration on other, more important things. Above the little group Tim Henman smiled and mouthed replies to an interviewer on Sky. Then a nurse came in and told them Mr Sandar hovered between life and death but they were doing all they could to save him.

Alice's expression was turned inward. A frown creaked her brow and she was unnaturally still.

'Why didn't you tell me before?' she asked Cynthia.

'I couldn't. Daddy wouldn't let me. He said he'd kill me if I breathed a word. And he meant it. I wanted to protect you. You were . . .' she searched for a word.

'So stupid!' Alice finished for her, shaking her head from side to side, her tone bitter. 'Such an idiot!'

'No, no. I was going to say, "an innocent"!' Cynthia told her.

'I trusted him,' Alice said, looking at Rudi. 'I believed it when Daddy said there were bad men after him.'

'No, Alice. Daddy was the bad man. He's

wanted by the police in England. They can't pin anything on him. They've no proof. But he's hated there. Someone would kill him if he went back there.'

'And to think I never guessed. What an imbecile you must think me!'

'Someone has already tried to kill him,' Rudi said. 'They may have succeeded.'

'I thought he was the goodie. You know, Harrison Ford. Mel Gibson. *They,* these hunters were, I thought, the wicked ones. The men in black, you know, Tommy Lee Jones, following, following, persecuting my darling Daddy and that's why we had to be careful.' She sniffed, tossed her head, standing there in her bloodstained beaded gown. 'I *enjoyed* being careful. Obeying Daddy's orders. Doing as I was told. "Don't ever go off alone," he told me. "Stay with Kalo." Instructions like that, making me think he treasured me. It never occurred to me that he could be the evil one, that he . . .' her voice broke and Rudi put a gentle hand on her shoulder. She turned to him blindly and he embraced her shivering body, soothing her as her mother had moments before.

A doctor came and stood before them. His eyes were tired. 'He's out of danger,' he said, 'I think he is going to be all right.'

'Mrs Sandar, let me take Alice home.' Rudi looked at Cynthia anxiously. 'She's cold and shivering. She's had a shock.'

'No.' Alice looked up at him. 'I have to stay, to find out for sure.'

'Sweetheart, it's best you go. They've said he is stable. I'll stay here.' Cynthia sighed wearily. 'Let Rudi take you. Kalo is outside. Have a sleep. Rest.'

'I couldn't,' Alice was adamant. 'I have to see it through.'

'No. You come with me. Your father's asleep. Nothing will happen until morning. You'll just sit here dozing, achieving nothing. You're exhausted. Come along, my love.' Rudi was persuasive. 'A hot bath and a warm drink and rest.'

Cynthia nodded vigorously. 'It's nearly morning,' she said, echoing Rudi. 'Nothing will happen until morning. You need to get out of that dress.'

'All right. But you'll telephone if . . .'

'If there's any change, yes, of course. I promise. Now take her, Rudi.'

'We'll be back before lunch,' Alice told her mother who nodded.

She allowed Rudi to lead her down the cold antiseptic corridors of the hospital into the pale silver dawning. She was not prepared for the battery of flashing bulbs, the press, the paparazzi, the mass of people waiting outside for them as they pushed their way to the car, Kalo making a path for them.

'Is he dead?'

*'Il est mort?'*

153

'Is Victor Sandar dead at last?'

'How is the villain? Why are they bothering to try to save him?'

'He should suffer like his victims!'

'Is the bastard—'

'Who shot him?'

'Whoever it was deserves a medal!'

And a voice calling, 'Wolfe, Wolfe, you got an exclusive?'

'Just like you, Rudi! In at the kill.'

She heard them, a cacophony of shrill voices, the smelly press of bodies that had been sweating there all night in the heat too close to her, and she nearly fainted. But Rudi was supporting her and Kalo was opening the limo door, shielding her. He used his bulk to shoulder aside the pressing crowd of journalists and photographers. He almost shoved the girl and her companion into the car. As Rudi fell into the seat beside her his eyes met those of the burly Korean and what he saw there made him shiver. Kalo's eyes were cold and hostile and very threatening.

It was only momentary, this exchange of glances, then he slammed the car door shut and screened out the curious. He got into the front seat and drove them back to the villa in silence.

# CHAPTER SIXTEEN

'Make love to me, Rudi.'

She came into the guest bedroom where he lay fully clothed on the bed. He had not taken his clothes off in case he was needed suddenly to go out again, back to the hospital.

Kalo had shown him where to go. The huge chauffeur had led him to one of the guest rooms on the far side of the villa, away from the master bedroom and Alice's suite. Kalo told him he could crash there until morning.

He exuded menace and although he said nothing at all Rudi could feel his hostility in his every move.

Before he left Rudi alone he leaned forward and whispered sibilantly, 'What they mean, you gotta exclusive? You hurt anyone here, you're dead,' turned, and left. Rudi, after his experiences in Bosnia, was sanguine about his own death so the Korean's bluster did not upset him.

He took off his jacket and threw himself on the bed. He lay there, hands clasped behind his head, speculating on the situation. Kalo suspected who he was and it would not be long before he told someone. Well, Rudi decided, he could not worry about that now.

He must have dozed off as outside the world faintly stirred into life. Then he heard the door open and turning his head he saw her there, a white towel around her, her hair wet from the shower. She was scrubbed clean and she looked very beautiful, very ethereal, a golden girl with golden hair, golden eyes and skin.

He knew how perfect her body was, how each muscle and ligament, each crevice and curve blended into a wondrous whole. He'd seen the vision that night when he'd watched from the tree.

'Make love to me please,' she whispered and sat beside him, letting the towel fall off, pressing her damp face into the hollow of his neck.

He leapt up as if scalded. 'Alice, no!' he cried, shocked.

'Oh Rudi, I need you. I need you now.'

He took her by the shoulders and shook her gently. His mouth was dry and he had trouble getting the words out.

'Alice, listen. You're in shock. It's been an awful night. You're asking me to do this because you want to escape. You want to deaden the pain of the realisation of the truth about your father. Don't you see?'

She nodded, to his surprise agreeing with him.

'Yes. Yes, I do. You are right. So, what's wrong with that? I want you to hold me, love me, make me feel better. Grown up. What does it matter?'

'It matters to me. I won't take advantage of you. I love you. I don't want to . . . to seduce you on the worst night of your life.'

'*I'm* seducing *you*,' she interpolated with a trace of a smile.

'I don't want you to use me like a drug. To forget reality for a while. I would always remind you of the horror of tonight.'

'You will anyway. Wouldn't it be better if there was some . . . beautiful *healing* in this night? Oh, my darling, darling, Rudi. From the first moment I saw you I wanted you. I knew immediately you were the one. Oh love me, love me now.'

Heat rose from her body where before it had been cold. She pressed him back on the bed kissing him passionately and, instantly aroused, he could not help kissing her back. She tasted of shampoo and bath oil and sex. He wanted to be absorbed by her body, he ached to become part of her forever. He felt incomplete without her. He needed to feel her against his bare flesh, her flesh stroking his flesh. He desired her, mind, body and soul and as he pulled off his clothes he sighed as skin touched skin and scorching fiery body bound to body in a sublime union, at home at last, complete.

She was a virgin. The discovery did not surprise him, yet she was eager and innovative, not passive at all and he coaxed her, urged her, encouraged her to climax.

'I love you, Alice. Oh Christ, how I love you,' he told her and she smiled a little secret smile.

'I know,' she whispered, 'I know.'

She lay in his arms. All the life and luminosity had returned, all her vitality was there again and she sighed and kissed him.

'Oh my God, I never knew . . . I never believed . . .' She rose and almost floated to the door and locked it.

'I forgot,' she laughed over her shoulder at him, putting her finger to her lips, 'Kalo,' she murmured. 'I left the radio on in my room.' She tapped her forehead and grinned at him, 'He'll think I'm there. He's not the brightest of men.' She was like a child in her glee. She came back to him and pulled the sheets off him. 'Now ravish me again,' she instructed, sliding in beside him, the velvety length of her golden body on his. 'And again. And again. I want it all. All of you, my dearest, dearest darling. I want to drown in you.'

It was lunchtime when she left him, sated, full of the wonder of her love, intoxicated by the mysteries of her body, bemused by the revelation of herself, her generosity. He showered and dressed, feeling out of place in his evening clothes. His body felt languid and strangely numb as if all his nerve ends had been drugged.

He heard her call, 'Kalo. Kalo. Tell Mr Wolfe I'll wait for him in the living-room.'

There was mischief and gaiety in her voice. Kalo, Rudi realised, would guess that something had happened but he would not know what.

Then there was a knock at his door and Rudi heard the chauffeur's voice. 'Mr Wolfe, there is food below. Then we go to the hospital.'

Rudi hurried down the floating staircase into the sunlit room below. He stopped when he saw her there and when she turned to him her beauty struck him like a blow. She wore cream silk trousers with a brown leather belt and a white tee shirt, a brown leather bag slung over her shoulder. Her hair was pulled back and held in a barrette at the nape of her neck, her face scrubbed. Her skin glowed biscuit-beige and her eyes sparkled. But her glance was anxious and searched his across the room. She wore a heavy necklace of amber beads around her neck and gold nuggets in her ears. She smiled at him and her smile was strained.

'Have some food,' she said, a trifle uncertainly. 'You must be starving.'

There was a feast laid out on the low marble table; cold meats, langoustine and crab, salad, warm crusty bread, cheeses and wine, fruit and crudités.

'I'm ashamed, oh Rudi, I'm so ashamed . . .'

His heart plummeted. 'Oh God, I told you you'd regret . . . Oh, I warned you . . .'

But she was shaking her head vehemently. 'Oh no! No. Because I'm so hungry! I'm ashamed because I'm starving. One shouldn't be hungry, not *this* hungry when Daddy—' She suddenly choked on the words and burst into sobs.

He took her in his arms and held her close as the storm broke and she cried her anguish and bewilderment out. She knew he understood, empathised and she let the healing deluge dampen his jacket as he soothed her, rocked her in his embrace.

'I've had a terrible thought, Rudi.' She turned her tear-drenched face up to him. 'That I knew all the time, about Dadda. That deep down,' she gulped, 'I *guessed*. But I was too much of a wimp to face up to it. I didn't *want* to believe it. Refused to. I protected myself, guarded myself from hearing the truth. I deliberately closed my ears to gossip and innuendo, to the rumours. I refused to listen. When Mummy said that last night,' she grimaced, 'it was like her saying something I already knew but wouldn't acknowledge. Like, I wasn't surprised.'

She sniffed and at that moment Kalo came into the room carrying a silver pot of coffee. He stared into Rudi's eyes but this time his gaze was not so hostile. He put the coffee down and said, 'Here are tissues.'

Rudi nearly laughed at the banality of it. At the worst moments of our lives we need

160

tissues.

'You hurt her, I'll kill you,' Kalo whispered and Rudi, glancing at him, saw he meant it.

Having made his position clear, Kalo seemed to relax somewhat. 'I'll wait outside. In the car,' he said.

Alice's storm had subsided into hiccups and little jagged breaths. Rudi persuaded her to eat and they both managed, with the help of a little wine and a cup of coffee, to fill their stomachs.

She touched him all the time. She seemed to need to reassure herself that he was still there, he was real, he was part of her. She needed to remind herself of the reality of their love. When their eyes met it was like lovemaking, arousing them both with fleeting memories of their passionate union, rekindling that passion.

They drove to the hospital and found that Cynthia had not moved. She sat where they had left her in the alcove, the television screen above her still silently flickering, flashing images of Coca-Cola, Cantona, Rusedski, an endless parade of sports personalities following each other. At the moment Damon Hill was saying something and every so often a shot of him holding a cup aloft was flashed on the screen.

'How is he?' Alice hurried to her mother and Rudi felt a sickening sense of separation as she removed herself physically and mentally from him.

'He'll pull through,' Cynthia replied listlessly. Rudi thought she seemed disappointed.

'That's good, Mummy. Isn't it? Good?'

'I don't know,' she murmured. 'You just don't know.'

'Oh Mummy, can't we just forget the . . .' Alice squirmed 'The . . . past. The other. It was years ago—'

'No. No, Alice. Now I've told you I'll not have you fudging the truth. You cannot avoid it any longer. You can't file it away, pretend it isn't important.' She was shredding a tissue between her fingers. 'It's happening *now*. He's got people working for him as we speak, *his* people as he calls them. Thugs. Terror merchants.'

Alice had put her hands over her ears.

'You're exaggerating', she cried. 'I know you are. Just because Daddy's not—' She shook her head violently. 'I'm *happy*, Mummy. I don't want anything to stop this joy I feel. Daddy's getting better. It will all be all right.' She glanced at Rudi, then at Cynthia. 'I'll talk to him, ask him and he'll never do anything bad again. You'll see. I'll persuade him.'

Cynthia's eyes met Rudi's helplessly over Alice's head. He saw her dilemma, her exasperation. She would be forever torn between trying not to hurt Alice and telling the unvarnished truth. She shrugged her shoulders

162

and gave up.

They sat in silence until a nurse came and told them they could go in now and see the patient. Cynthia noticed her daughter's instant gravitation towards Rudi Wolfe, the way her hand sought his and buried itself confidently in his fist. She knew then what had happened between them and rejoiced. She smiled to herself. At least something was right with the world and perhaps, just maybe, the mother prayed, Rudi Wolfe would be Alice's salvation.

\*         \*         \*

Victor Sandar burned with murderous rage. His beloved daughter stood at the side of his hospital cot hanging onto the young whipper-snapper he'd seen her get out of the car with the night before. She was all over the guy. And Cynthia looked benignly upon them. Smug and self-satisfied. He wanted to leap out of the bed and strangle her. He wanted to scream 'Take your hands offa her' to that tall young man whose proprietorial manner with his daughter was driving him crazy. But he was in no position to do anything at all, hooked up as he was to all sorts of tubes and machines and apparatus.

'There must be rumours flying about,' he told his wife. 'Get Eddie on the phone. Here's the number. I wrote it down for you. Tell him I'm fine. Tell him go on as normal.'

'Murdering people?'

He turned, startled, at the sound of his daughter's voice. The soft tone she used to talk to him with had vanished and she sounded cold and harsh.

'No, pet. What makes you think that?'

'Mummy said . . .'

There was murder in the look he gave Cynthia but he made a supreme effort to collect himself and his voice was bland as he replied, 'Mamma exaggerates. Of course I have to do things I don't like. No one gets to the top, Alice, unless they are ruthless. Presidents and politicians, business tycoons and rich men all have skeletons buried, I promise you. They have to be single-minded and in control.' He took her hand in his, drawing her away from Rudi, looking deeply into her eyes as if he wanted to mesmerise her. 'But I've never, never in my life murdered anyone, ever. Do you believe me?'

She nodded, 'Oh yes.'

He looked at his wife and daughter as the nurse came in to ask them to leave, ignoring Rudi completely. He patted the bed. 'Sit here, my dearest,' he told Alice. Obediently she sat.

'Now listen to me,' he said. 'I have never murdered anyone. I swear before God. But there are people in this world who think I have.' His eyes darted to Cynthia's anguished face. 'Ask your mother. Go on, ask her. Ask her if I murdered anyone.'

'No. You haven't personally, Victor,' Cynthia said coldly. 'But you have ordered—'

'Quiet!' It was the first time he had raised his voice. 'Quiet!' he told Cynthia then he turned to Alice. 'See. I told you. Now go home, sweetheart. Remember, don't believe all you hear.'

She rose and kissed his forehead.

'You're my baby, Alice, and I love you. No one will ever love you the way I do. Remember that.'

'I will.'

'And don't talk to the press,' he instructed. 'That's a very important thing, my darling. They are evil. They invent things.' She nodded. Rudi shrank back against the wall as if trying to make himself invisible.

## CHAPTER SEVENTEEN

The girl, Amber, seemed unconscious. When Martin woke up he saw that she was curled up on the bare floor in a foetal position. When he touched her she rolled over and he saw she'd been sick on the floor.

'Amber? Amber? You all right?'

He was frightened. It was all very well fantasising about how he would kill Victor Sandar and quite another matter to have actually pulled the trigger. It had all happened

165

so quickly and now he was on the run. And this girl, his alibi, lay on the floor, alarmingly cold, like a dead thing.

He could feel her pulse though. He shivered when he thought: suppose, just suppose she was dead and he was arrested for the wrong murder. Wouldn't that be ironic? Serve him right!

He sat on the bed thinking. Her name, he knew, was Amber Crosbie and she had a brother called Roger. That much he was sure of but not much else. He also knew that the villa he'd been in the night before was owned by people called Crawley and their son, a friend of Amber's, was called Jonathan. He'd climbed a tree in their garden overlooking the Sandar place and from that tree he'd shot Victor Sandar. Every time he thought of it he was shaken to his very foundations by hatred, triumph, fear and disbelief.

After some thought he went downstairs to the phone in the hall. After a lot of frustrating mistakes he found the Crawley number, dialled it and asked to speak to Jonathan Crawley. He finally got through.

'Hey, hey, that you Rudi? Hey, hey old buddy.' Jonathan's voice greeted Martin without preamble.

'No, no. I'm Amber and Roger's friend. I'm, er, their cousin.'

They'd decided on this the previous night. 'Roger and I can say you're our cousin. He'll back me, Roger will. He'll wish he had the courage to do what you did. Execute the bastard.'

'Oh!' Martin could almost hear Jonathan at the other end of the phone, thinking, trying to place him. Failing.

'Is Roger there?' Martin asked. 'Amber wants him.' He thought of the comatose girl on the floor upstairs. There was a pause at Jonathan's end and Martin could hear him muttering, 'Oh Christ!' in a resigned tone.

'She out of it again?' he asked.

'Yeah!'

'Okay. Gotcha. Got the picture. Amber's done it again.'

'Yeah.'

'Roger's with the Fontaines. They went there after the party. You got the number?'

'Somewhere. Oh hell, I left it . . .' he pretended he was searching.

'N'mind, it's in front of me here.' Jonathan read it out as Martin scribbled it on the yellow wall which was already thick with numbers, obscene messages, hearts and flowers and cryptic comments.

The phone was slippery in his hands. The hall, naked of any kind of decoration, simmered damply in the heat. It stank mustily. The concierge went out, passing him by, leaving in her wake the aroma of stale booze, cigarettes and perspiration.

When he finally got through to Roger he

simply told him his sister needed him and gave him the address, begging him to come at once.

'She okay?' Roger asked without hope.

'I don't know,' Martin replied and the phone clicked. Martin went back upstairs where he found Amber exactly as he'd left her. He sat on the side of his bed and waited.

Roger arrived about half an hour later. He came bursting into the mean little room, hardly acknowledging Martin's presence. He yanked Amber to her feet and walked her up and down the room, slapping her face. He forced some coffee he'd brought in a polystyrene container into her. He pinched the backs of her legs and finally, when she appeared to be regaining some semblence of life he began to clean her up.

He seemed irritated with Martin, as if the latter should have known what to do, and he spoke to him sharply.

'Go down to the nearest shop and buy a pair of jeans and a tee,' he said. 'She can't go out like this.' Amber was still in her ballgown which was crumpled and stained. She looked like a neglected doll and flopped about, her limbs uncoordinated.

Martin did as he was told. He was glad enough to get out of the building, breathe the sea air. He wandered along the narrow street. His mind was a carousel of emotions and feelings swirling around inside his head.

All his life he'd stayed close to home,

isolated with his mother, leading a quiet life, and now he'd suddenly been thrust into a maelstrom of activity with strangers. He felt confused and disorientated. So he channelled his thoughts to the task at hand and found a boutique with rails of tee shirts outside.

He had trouble about her size, but he found a girl who seemed to him about Amber's build and he got the jeans and tee shirt in the size she recommended. He returned to the room wondering about the situation he had got himself into but acknowledging that he had no choice. The girl was his alibi.

She was fully awake and sat shivering and shaking in her bra and pants. Roger's manner towards Martin had changed completely on his return. He rose from the bed where he had been sitting beside his sister and greeted him effusively, pumping Martin's hand enthusiastically, as if, Martin thought, it was some kind of game, a fantasy, like a movie, this murder of Victor Sandar.

'Good God, man, why didn't you say? You're a hero, for Christ's sake.'

Amber pulled on the jeans and tee, yanking off the tabs with trembling impatient hands.

Roger said, 'Let's go and get some breakfast. Get outta this tip.'

They all went down to the nearest café.

Roger was electric with excitement. He could hardly contain himself. He kept punching Martin's shoulder, leaning across the table, giving him affectionate little pats and jabs and saying, 'Good on you!'

They told him the whole story.

'What did you do with the gun?' he asked.

'We threw it in the water in Golfe Juan,' Amber said. 'It's heavy. It'll stay there, at the bottom.'

'No fingerprints on it?' he asked.

Martin said, 'Might be a blurred one.'

Amber shook her head. 'No, no,' she cried. 'I wiped it thoroughly. Really polished it clean.'

Her eyes had regained some life but she shook all the time. Her lips were dry and she sweated profusely. Her skin was yellow, like a corpse.

'Good,' Roger nodded. 'There's nothing to connect you with any of it.'

'I thought he was a contract killer,' Amber told her brother, giggling. Then she began to hug her shaking body, wrapping her arms around herself. Martin wanted to hold her, make her better, warm her into relaxation. He had never felt so protective before.

Roger glanced around at the people at the other tables and the crowd swirling around them but no one was paying any attention to them. He slid a small packet across the table to his sister. 'Take it. You need it.'

Her eyes lit up and she grabbed the plastic packet and fled to the door marked 'Dames'.

'God, I'm glad you've done this thing,'

Roger told Martin for the umpteenth time, making no reference to the little incident that had just occurred. 'See, he's not just destroyed Mother and Father, but the whole family. She's'—he jerked his head backwards in the direction that Amber had gone—'been on that stuff since Mother . . .' His bottom lip trembled and he bit it fiercely, chewing it, then continued. 'I just wish I'd had the courage.' He stared out to sea. Children's shrieks and the laughter of adults blended with the roar of the waves. People passed, linking arms, licking ice-creams. Pretty young girls in bikinis and sarongs flirted with handsome tanned boys and striped umbrellas gave cheerful shade to prone near-naked bodies. A few groups were barbecueing sausages on the beach and the acrid smoke reached them in occasional puffs. It was a happy, carefree scene but Roger's face did not blend with it.

'It's been hell,' he told Martin. 'Sheer hell.'

Martin nodded, 'I know', he said and Roger focused on him.

'Yes of course you do,' he replied.

When Amber returned to the table she was calm and slightly abstracted, as if her strung-out nerves had been anaesthetised. But at least she was alert.

'Okay?' Roger asked as she sat down.

'Oh yes,' she nodded.

They sat for a while in silence. Amber stared around idily watching the passing

171

crowd. Then they heard her gasp. They looked at her and saw that her eyes had widened in alarm. She pointed, wagging her finger wordlessly.

'What? What is it?' Roger cried, alarmed.

'Oh God, look!'

'What?'

They followed her gaze. A man sat near them drinking espresso and reading his paper, *Le Figaro*. The headlines screamed something in French that Martin could not understand but the name Victor Sandar leapt out at him.

'What is it? What does it say?'

The brother and sister exchanged glances. Then Amber looked at him and dropped the bombshell.

'He's not, dead!' she announced, looking at Martin in dismay. 'He's recovering. In hospital. Victor Sandar's not dead. The bastard didn't die. You didn't kill him. He's still alive.'

## CHAPTER EIGHTEEN

Amber's world was darkening, the boundaries shrinking, the avenues of possibility diminishing dramatically. Her world now revolved around fixes and the availability of her stuff and where and when she'd get her next score. That was her world and it was closing in on her.

There was for her no interest in boys, dancing, discos, food, love, sex, flirtation, shopping, sport, swimming, clothes, gossip, chats, friends. People in general were ignored by her: didn't exist or received only the most cursory and superficial attention. Her mind was elsewhere. Her habit was a jealous mistress; it absorbed her night and day. All she thought about, lived for, breathed, desired was the next score to quiet her nerves, her stomach, her driven mind, her tortured and restless soul, her central disturbed being. To get the stuff, to quiet the riot inside, the constant chatter of her nerves, the fear. To anaesthetise the hyper-sensitive pulsating centre of her for a moment, to be still. To quiet for minutes, an hour, a night if she could find the right mix, the perfect cocktail of uppers and downers that might control her throbbing tension. To float, untroubled and semi-comatose, that was all that preoccupied her night and day.

That and her resentment of Victor Sandar who had brought her to this. He was her beloved obsession.

She felt sorry for herself, that she had become this semi-living zombie. She reached out for her father, the voice in her head calling to him, 'Help me! Help me!' But he wasn't there any more like he used to be when she was little and it seemed to her he could fix anything, still any storm, cure everything. He was gone. He'd left them, deserted them, all because of Victor Sandar. He'd shot himself. Committed suicide.

She had this terrible fear that he was not able to pray for her, care for her from a better place. Others prayed to the dead and the happy peaceful departed soul sent down a benediction, a blessing. But her father was probably in hell and couldn't help. Lost for eternity.

The nuns had told her suicides were damned forever though she often wondered how they knew for sure. But she did know suicides were damned.

She had been with her mother when they found her father. The study door had been locked which was unusual and the key still in the other side. Her mother had to poke it out with a hair clip, then unlock the door with her own key. Amber had been just behind her when she'd flung the door open and they'd seen him hanging over the chair, half his head missing, blood and brains spattered everywhere. Her mother had tried to cover Amber's eyes but it was too late. The hideous scene was seared into her memory forever. It came out to haunt her every night. Unless she was stoned.

Roger had been spared that. That was why she had to take stuff and he was merely angry.

Their mother had broken down after that.

Her nerves had given way and she lived on Librium during the day and Mogadon at night. But even that was not enough and bit by bit their mother got more and more disturbed and remote. As time passed she became terribly confused and eventually she had to be confined. Sectioned. After that she was utterly passive because, Amber believed, they filled her with Largactil. She plumped out into an unrecognisable egg-shape, no longer their lovely mother, a stranger. Eventually, permanently institutionalised, she seemed quiet, and if not content, at least unworried.

Sometimes she did not recognise her children. She sat in a chair in the common-room and stared vacantly out into the gardens or rested on a bench in the grounds and gazed glassily at the far-off hills. Roger and Amber hurried to see her, always sure that this time, *this* time she'd know them, be the mother they remembered, bright-eyed, full of life, her arms open to them, eager to hold them to her heart.

But she never was. Victor Sandar had made sure of that. He'd quenched the flame of love and life within her and she withered visibly before their eyes. Sadly, with infinite regret, they let her slip away from them and clung to each other for the only comfort available to them. Amber had her drugs and Roger had his anger.

Then this fellow had appeared, an ordinary-looking chap but an avenging angel no less.

175

He'd shot the man the brother and sister had cast as Mephisthophelean pure evil. The man who had destroyed their lives and who lived next to the Crawleys on the beautiful Côte d'Azur, and seemed to have a charmed and opulent existence, until now in no way suffering for what he had done, the pain he had caused.

For a little while they had rejoiced. Justice had been done. Only now it seemed the villain had not died. He lived on, indestructable.

The three whispered together and discovered they were all of them of a single mind.

'He can't be let off!' Roger decided. 'Not now. It has to be finished.'

'I messed up,' Martin moaned. 'I bloody messed up.'

'No. You did good,' Amber insisted. 'You nearly succeeded.'

Roger bought a paper. They sat perusing it intently.

'It says here: "he hovered between life and death all night",' Amber said. 'That's something.'

'We didn't have your guts,' Roger said sadly to Martin.

'I'll have to try again,' Martin told them. He was not sure that that was what he wanted to do but felt it was expected of him.

'We'll help,' Amber said. 'This time we'll be in there with you.'

'But we'll have to be careful. Security will be tightened,' Martin told them.

'It will be more difficult,' Roger said. 'They'll be on the lookout.'

'They'll be after me,' Martin told them.

'I said, they don't have a clue to your identity.' Amber sounded impatient.

'You don't understand. There's a guy in London. Eddie. He'll know I left London. He'll put two and two together eventually. Bound to.'

They were silent for a while, then Martin said, 'I've got no gun now.'

'We'll think of something.'

'There's one at the Fontaines',' Amber remarked. 'It would be dead easy to steal it.'

The sun scorched the pavements now and the heat rose in cloudy vapours off the sea. People were wilting, their ices melting. Sweating men were dragging whining redfaced children behind them to their air-conditioned rooms for a siesta. Customers outside the cafés slumped, legs apart, fanning themselves with the menus. A helicopter put-putted past in the robin's-egg-blue sky waving an advertisement on a banner behind it.

'There are so many ways to kill him, if we can just get near him,' Amber said.

'No. There are not!' Martin sounded irritated. 'Do what? Can you see me strangling him? Poisoning him? Knifing him? Don't be daft! There's only one way.'

Amber shrugged. 'Maybe,' she said, then, 'If only you hadn't missed.'

'I know.' Martin banged his fist on the table. 'But I *didn't* miss. The wound wasn't fatal is all.'

'In the meantime you have to be Martin Crosbie,' Roger decided. 'No one must get your name. Certainly not the press.'

'Agreed.'

'You're our cousin,' Amber confirmed. 'But best keep a low profile. Not mix too freely with the gang. You might give yourself away.'

'No one suspects me at all,' Martin said. He was fed up with what he thought of as the Crosbies' silliness. They seemed to have no sense in their reasoning, leaping about from plan to plan. But he wanted to be near Amber and he needed her for his alibi.

'The police don't even know you exist. Anyhow you were with me.' Amber smiled at him. 'If they do discover you, question you, all you have to do is say we were snogging. I'll back you up—then they've no proof.'

'Except Eddie the Ferret in London,' Martin said.

'What can he do? The police won't listen to him.'

'He can get on a plane.' Martin glared at her. 'God, don't be stupid! He'll tell Victor Sandar and I'm much more afraid of what *he'll* do than I am of the police.'

'But he doesn't know what you look like.

You said they haven't seen you for a long time. You're Martin Crosbie now.'

'Will they try to hurt your mother?' Roger asked.

Martin shook his head. 'No. She's in hospital. But they won't hurt her. She's a woman. It's their code of ethics.'

Roger snorted and made a face. 'Ethics!' he muttered.

'Look, we'll change your appearance,' Amber said.

'They'll not expect you to be with us. No one looking for you would think you'd be in our set.'

'We'll dye your hair blond.'

'Jesus, do you have to?'

Amber nodded and Roger said, 'You can borrow some of my clothes. My stuff is pretty *sportif*. South of France fashion. They'll not expect that either. With blond hair, fake tan on your face—properly done, the way you have it now you look jaundiced! A blazer with a pink shirt and cream trews; you'll be unrecognisable. Promise!' Roger was laughing now, excited, involved in an adventure.

They talked, ordered a burger and chips, felt the adrenalin rush as they drank coffee and mulled over what they should do, what they could do. They were heated and impractical and Martin began to have serious misgivings about including them in any plan. They were too irresponsible, too hot-headed.

They'd be hopeless in a crisis. Yet, he reminded himself, Amber had conducted herself with remarkable aplomb when the chips had been down.

They were relieved to talk to each other. All these years they had built up a huge resentment against Victor Sandar and it was good to share their experiences with each other.

They sat there until night fell over the Côte d'Azur and the lights came sparkling on and the music started its steady beat and the sea darkened to an opaque slate-grey, then black. It whispered sibilantly as a background to their talk.

They returned reluctantly to Martin's small room where they slept innocently intertwined, fully dressed, the three of them on the bed holding onto each other, preparing for tomorrow and the many plans to be made—including the transformation of Martin Sloane.

## CHAPTER NINETEEN

Victor Sandar remained in hospital for seven days and nights. Cynthia, fully cognisant of the situation between her daughter and Rudi Wolfe, invited him to stay in the guest room.

'You might as well, Rudi. You take Alice to the hospital each day so it is more convenient.

Obviously.'

She pretended ignorance of the true state of affairs, but she was very happy about the situation.

The servants were nonplussed. Aware of what was happening, they were bemused by their mistress' total acceptance of the nightly comings and goings in the villa, the nocturnal traffic from room to room.

Nana was outraged. She puffed and blew and radiated disapproval but Cynthia purposefully ignored her reaction and fielded her derogatory comments dexterously. She could not expect the servant to understand the fact that Alice had been saved from a very tricky situation.

Only Kalo remained impartial and no one knew what he thought. He obeyed all orders impassively.

Every night Alice crept down the corridor to her lover's arms and remained there until morning. She was the only one who was totally unaware that anyone knew what she was doing.

'You are the core of my heart, my love.'

'I know. Blessed, blessed girl.'

'Without you I could not live, Rudi. I love you so much.'

She was not conscious of the fact that Cynthia knew what she was doing. Alice knew that she was aware that they were in love but it did not dawn on her that she was happily turning a blind eye.

181

Alice had been saved. Cynthia didn't much care whether this was true love or not; all she knew was that Victor couldn't get her daughter now. Not any more. Alice had gone down the path of passion and love with this young man, too far to be lured back into childish unquestioning adoration of her father. It was not now a possibility.

Cynthia daily breathed sighs of relief. Alice was discovering love and sex with a beautiful young man who obviously loved her. That was as it should be. A bridge had been crossed; Alice's loss of virginity had put her out of the reach of her father.

Cynthia's only regret was that Victor had not died. It would have simplified things for them all. Alice need not have had her nose rubbed in her father's criminal activities and she, his wife, could be free of him at last. She feared only what he would do when he found out the truth about Alice.

They visited the hospital every day. Cynthia advised Rudi not to go into his room with them.

'It will aggravate him and he might try to split you two up,' she told the couple. 'Best he's ignorant that you love each other, at least for a while.'

'He'll know when he comes home,' Alice stated firmly. 'That we see each other, I mean. I'm not going to lie to him, Mamma. I don't see why I should.'

'I can't stay at the villa when he returns,' Rudi said.

Alice frowned. 'I suppose it wouldn't be the thing,' she admitted regretfully.

'Never mind. We'll arrange something.' Cynthia reassured them.

'She knows I love you,' Alice told Rudi, but he didn't reply.

On the seventh day Victor Sandar was discharged. Alice insisted that Rudi accompany her to the hospital.

'I need you with me. I'm not going to pretend,' she told him firmly. 'I want Daddy to get used to you. Oh, he'll huff and he'll puff at first but whatever he's done, I love him and he loves me.' She looked apologetically into Rudi's eyes and he saw there her desperation. Loyalty was one of her cardinal virtues and she would not give up the idea of her father as a wronged man. A man about whom they exaggerated.

'I can't be without you for a second,' she whispered to him.

So he remained in the foyer while Cynthia and Alice went to Victor's room and fetched him to check him out of the hospital.

He was pushed to the entrance in a wheelchair by a white-coated porter followed by Cynthia and Alice, Rudi falling into place behind them, close to his love.

As they emerged into the blinding sunlight they were faced by the buzzing mass of paparazzi, popping flashlights and barking questions.

'You OK, Victor?'

'Who was it tried to blow you away? You any idea?'

'Know what it feels like now, Victor?'

Victor Sandar snarled at them as they pressed in on him. Kalo was trying to protect him as they made their way to the limousine and Rudi's car. Then an English voice shouted, 'You bought the story, Rudi? You gotta deal with the devil?'

Then another, 'Exclusive rights, Rudi? This better than Yugoslavia, or worse?'

Victor was picked up by Kalo and deposited in the limousine. He turned his head and stared at the man at his daughter's side. His eyes were black pools of venom.

'What do they mean, Rudi?' Alice's wide-eyed glance shamed Rudi as they hurried to his car but he did not reply.

Victor gestured to Kalo shouting, 'Alice! Come here! Come with us!' As Rudi banged the door he heard the raucous shout, 'Alice, come here at once!' but he started the engine and paid no attention to Victor's calls.

When they were underway she asked him again, 'What did those newspapermen mean, Rudi?'

He sighed, his eyes on the road, then reluctantly he tried to explain. 'I better come clean,' he said. 'As I told you, I'm a journalist.

They think I'm doing a story on your father.'

He waited for her to digest this piece of information.

'You said you were a writer . . . I thought—'

'Books! Yes, I understand. But I did say I covered a war.'

Glancing sideways at her he saw the struggle in her face. There was silence as they drove along behind the limousine.

'Forgive me,' she said. 'I didn't quite get that you were *that* kind of writer. And were you going to write about Daddy?' she asked in a small voice.

He knew she was trying to accommodate the knowledge as she had tried to come to terms with the truth about her father, to absorb the information that was distasteful to her. It was unfair that she should have to accept all this disturbing news about the men she loved. They were being revealed as liars and cheats at worst, dissimulators at best, and she was struggling to find excuses to absolve the unpalatable truths about them.

'Have you trashed him? Exposed him?' she asked bitterly.

'How could I?' he enquired helplessly. 'I saw you that first night and fell madly in love.'

'Did you know who I was then?' she asked.

He was tempted to lie. He nearly said no but something in her eyes, the guileless request for truth forbade him.

'Yes. I knew.'

'So you were in that tree to . . . to—'—she bit her lip, trying to get the words out—'—spy on Daddy, not to see me?'

'No, no . . .' he sighed. 'Yes . . . I suppose. Only I *did* see you.'

'So you wanted to get to Daddy. Write all about him.'

'Yes. I was commissioned to do a piece on him. That was why I was in the South of France.'

There was a silence in the car, then she said, 'A nasty piece?'

'A truthful piece,' he said, than added, 'But I didn't. I couldn't.'

'Oh. Why not?'

'Good God, Alice, you know why not!' he cried.

'I don't think I know anything any more.' She sounded sad.

'I fell in love with you. Madly, passionately. How could I write something about your father that might hurt the one I loved? I wouldn't do that to you. You hold all the cards, my dearest one. I'll write nothing without your permission.'

She settled back silently and was quiet. He did not disturb her and said nothing more, giving her space. They cruised behind the limo through the crowded streets towards the villa.

Once on the Boulevard du Cap the limousine accelerated its pace and scorched the short distance to the house. No sooner had

186

the car pulled up than Victor Sandar erupted from it and, despite the fact that he was supposed to be an invalid, came charging towards Rudi's Audi and began yanking at the door.

'Get out, Alice, get out at once.' His face was brick-red, full of violent fury, and his daughter let her window down.

'Daddy . . .' she cried. 'Daddy, don't! Please! Listen.'

He tried to smash his fist through the closed window on Rudi's side, prowling around the car in feline-like movements. He began using his mobile phone as a weapon. The fury with which he attacked was murderous and Rudi could only watch helplessly as he bashed the phone again and again against the glass in mindless rage. The Perspex split slowly, little cobweb lines spreading to and fro through the pane.

Alice grabbed Rudi's arm, slipping her own through his, cowering against him. This was a man she did not know, this fiend at the window whose face was distorted and ugly. He was a stranger. The terrifying eyes frightened her and suddenly she saw that all the ugly facts she had not believed about him could be true.

'Daddy, Daddy, stop. Oh please, please stop.'

He circled the car shouting obscenities. Cynthia tried now and then to restrain him but he brushed her off roughly. He yanked open the door at his daughter's side and before Rudi could do anything to stop him he dragged her out onto the driveway and hauled her towards the villa.

Rudi jumped out of the car and he and Cynthia ran after them but his way was blocked by Kalo who simply put a heavy hand on his shoulder and propelled him back to his car. Cynthia went running into the house after them.

'This is family stuff,' Kalo said quietly. 'Beat it.'

Rudi saw Alice's shocked face turned to him as her father pushed her roughly into the house. It was a face full of tears, anguish and pleading. Cynthia was shouting, 'Let her go! Let her loose, you bastard.'

Kalo bent down. 'Go now. Get outta here.'

There was nothing Rudi could do. His beloved had disappeared inside the villa and the giant Korean's body blocked out the light and forbade disobedience. There was no way past him. Rudi accepted the inevitable, put his foot on the accelerator and roared away into the night.

## CHAPTER TWENTY

Alice's pillow was saturated. She had raged and cried, sobbed and shouted her anguish to the skies but to no avail. Locked in her room, the windows fastened, the keys gone, there was no escape for her. She had pounded on the walls, screamed for her mother, for Nana, but had only seen Kalo. He had brought her trays of food which she'd refused to eat and a message from her father.

'He say when you reasonable, miss, he'll talk to you. But you gotta come see him handcuffed to me.' Kalo's expression was regretful.

She turned a tearstained face to him and begged him, implored him to help her.

'Let me run away. Please, Kalo. Please. I'll never forget it if you do. Have pity on me, please.'

But Kalo refused. 'He kill me if I don' do as he say,' he told her. 'No, miss, you better do what he tell you. No good otherwise.'

'Will you take a note to Mr Wolfe then, Kalo. Please?'

But the driver shook his head. 'I don' wanna die,' he said. 'No way.'

She'd stared out of her barred, locked window onto her balcony and suddenly she'd seen him there. Rudi. In the tree. He'd climbed to the place where he'd first seen her and she gazed at him hopelessly. She pressed her palms against the window and stared at him with tragic eyes. His face was wild with pain and they gazed at each other, unable to touch, to hold onto each other in their aching longing, their anguish. They mouthed silent promises. 'I love you', they whispered, hopelessly, helplessly. Rudi was terrified he'd make it difficult for her, more painful for her if he interfered. He was terrified she'd be harmed by the father he now saw as a madman.

Cynthia railed at Victor, demanding he release her daughter.

'You fool! Don't you understand she'll hate you for this? You've thrown her into his arms, you idiot, and she'll never forgive you. Never.'

'Shut up, you bitch. Shut your mouth.'

He nearly struck her but barely stopped himself when he saw the expression in her eyes. He wouldn't listen. He didn't dare. He was jumpy, angry, fearful for his life, realising for the first time how close he had come to death, how all his safety systems had failed.

He could not figure out who had shot him and was aware that whoever it was would probably try again. His confidence was shaken, his paranoia aggravated and he too was a prisoner in his room, frightened to go out, terrified and vulnerable. He paced, unable to figure out why his world had turned upside down. He behaved like a cornered animal, unreasoning and panic-stricken.

He phoned Eddie but couldn't speak freely for he was sure the police were paying special attention to him at this moment in time. He was worried too in case Eddie and the boys thought he was losing it. Suppose they decided to take over? How could he prevent that? Although there was nothing forbidding his re-entry into England he was sure the French police had told Scotland Yard what had happened and the filth in England would use it as an excuse to take him in for questioning, make his life miserable. Oh, they'd be ever so nice, polite, but underneath they'd relish the opportunity to make things as unpleasant for him as they could. The bastards wouldn't be able to resist it.

So he had to put on a show of bravado and stay quietly in the villa and sit back and wait. And Victor Sandar was not good at waiting.

For what? He did not know and it was driving him mad. Nor had he the faintest idea how to deal with his daughter. Totally incapable of sympathy or subtlety or empathy, he was clueless. He had only ever obtained what he wanted by bribery or force so he had no clue how to manage Alice. He only knew one thing and that was whatever Cynthia advised he'd do the opposite. It never occurred to him that his wife would act solely in the interests of her daughter. He knew how Cynthia hated him and could not conceive of her unselfish concern for Alice. He believed, childishly, that anything she suggested would be aimed at upsetting him. This petty reasoning, if only he'd understood, was doing precisely what he did not want it to: driving a wedge between himself and his daughter.

'She'll see I'm right in the end,' he told himself. 'She loves me and will obey me.'

On the third day he sent for Kalo and told him to bring Alice to him.

'If you have to, *only* if you have to, mind, cuff her,' he told Kalo.

Kalo had to. She was like an eel and twice she almost got away, so he cuffed her. It was a wild-eyed woman who faced Victor Sandar in his office.

'You haven't been eating,' Victor said. She said nothing, simply stared at him across the desk. Her expression startled him. He'd never seen that look before on the face of his beloved child, though it was a look he'd seen on his wife's face many a time. Hostile. Angry. Contemptuous. No one looked at Victor Sandar with such utter contempt and got away with it. It shook him.

But this was his daughter, the child he adored and she had matured in some way since he had last looked into her eyes. He did not understand. She looked at him now, an adult to an adult, critical and, there it was, the expression he could not bear, contempt.

'All the things they whisper about you are true,' she said disdainfully. 'You've proved it.'

'I'm sending you away.' He could think of nothing else to do. It came to him suddenly that he had no choice, that she had grown out of childish punishments, that he'd have to take drastic action to maintain any hold on her. And dominate her he would.

'I'm sending you to Switzerland. You'll leave here early tomorrow morning. Kalo will drive you.'

'You can't do that!' she cried.

'Oh, but I can,' he replied coldly.

'I don't hate you, Daddy.' She hesitated, then corrected herself, 'Father. I only pity you.'

'You will communicate with no one before you go,' he told her.

'Wherever you send me I'll find him. He'll find me.' She was firm and cool.

'I don't think so,' he smiled. The icy eyes sent a chill up her spine. In spite of her brave words she was scared, but she would not give him the satisfaction of letting him see she was.

'You, my dear, are going to be incarcerated in an asylum. You'll be sectioned until I see fit to have you released. You'll soon learn to behave; you'll see. You'll not leave there until I'm satisfied you've learned your lesson.'

She could feel the scream rise inside her as Kalo led her out of the room and to her own where he took off the cuffs and locked her in once more. She stifled the scream and went to the window, but there was no one there. The tree rustled in the breeze from the sea and sighed and moved and the leaves quivered and whitened under the moon. But it remained empty.

And at the window the sad little ghostlike figure pressed a piece of white paper with the words 'HELP! HE'S SENDING ME TO SWITZERLAND. TO AN ASYLUM' printed on it.

All night long she stood there pressing the printed sign to the window, hoping against hope he would come. But the tree remained empty. There was no sign of anybody.

Morning broke and Alice, still in her nightie, was bundled into the Mercedes. Kalo drove the car swiftly away from the villa and down the Boulevard du Cap.

Cynthia later went to her daughter's room, found the crumpled piece of paper and read the message. She bent her head and wept.


## CHAPTER TWENTY-ONE

During the week they had gone through a long list of possibilities. It drove Martin Sloane mad. Their suggestions were bizarre and unrealistic and downright silly and several times he had to control himself or he would have screamed his annoyance at them.

They wanted to blow up the villa. They wanted to poison one of the bottles of wine that were delivered at intervals to the house.

'If we blow up the house we'll kill innocent people,' Martin pointed out. 'And unless you know about explosives you could take half the Cap with you.'

'Well, why should we care?' Roger was too hot-headed by half for Martin. He was worried that Amber and her brother did not know the meaning of the word caution.

At this point Amber was groggy and nervous, quite incapable of being any use to them at all. She was alternately indifferent, violently disposed to recklessness, apathetic and so full of hate she was explosive.

'They are all his people in there,' she cried. 'All tarred with the same brush. Why should we care about them? Blow up the whole lot of them, I say.'

Martin ground his teeth.

'I care about them,' he said adamantly. 'People work there. I'm not going to be like Victor Sandar, indifferent to others' suffering. I don't want to ruin some poor sod's life as he ruined mine by killing the one or ones he or she loves. It's not on.'

Martin's reservations were getting on Roger's nerves. 'Well, what's the objection to poisoning the wine?' he asked. Martin gave the same reason.

'Someone else might drink it,' he said. Roger repeated his total lack of sympathy for family, servants, staff or even friends of Victor Sandar.

'They deserve to be gone, man, even if they only visit him.'

'So that includes Jonathan's folks?' Martin asked. That shut him up for a while, but only a short while.

They watched from the Crawley's little guest house. The Crawleys had, in defiance of the Nice Corporation laws, built themselves a small guest house almost hidden by azaleas and hibiscus and liberally draped with bougainvillea and jasmine. It was at the bottom of their land and next to the Sandar villa. It was empty at the moment and the threesome tucked themselves in, squatting there to be close to the Sandar household. They watched. They talked. They plotted.

It was the only place where they could lurk and know they would not be seen by anyone in the villa near them. They could not get any nearer for the security in the *Villa Bella Vista* had become fortresslike. Dogs prowled, alarms went off if you so much as breathed close to them. There were electric currents in the barbed wire that ran over the tops of the walls separating the two households.

The group in the guest house kept the Venetian blinds a little way open so that they could see without being seen. Roger had called them over to the window when Kalo had brought the limousine with the tinted windows around to the entrance of the villa.

'Only Victor Sandar uses that car. The mother and daughter use the Merc or the Lexus. He must be coming out. Maybe we

196

could do something . . .' Amber cried.

'Don't even think about it,' Martin cautioned. 'Not unless you're desperate to spend tonight in a French jail.'

Martin was becoming more and more exasperated by them. He was meticulous and careful and they were wild and totally lacked discretion. But Amber *was* his alibi. They had changed his appearance and now he fitted unremarkably into the group they belonged to and did not stick out like a sore thumb. When they had brought him to the guest house, the servants in the Crawleys', used to the comings and goings of Jonathan's friends and familiar with the Crosbies, made no objection. Did not raise an eyebrow. Martin was well aware that if he had been on his own before his transformation this would not have been the case. There was no way he could have hidden out in the guest house without Amber and Roger and his changed appearance.

And he was glad enough to have someone to share his hatred of Victor Sandar with. To be able to talk about the enemy, give vent to venom and know they were of like mind.

They watched, fascinated, as the girl was dragged out of the house.

'Good grief!' Martin gazed in disbelief. 'It's prehistoric.'

'In chains!' Amber breathed in wide-eyed astonishment. 'Christ, she's handcuffed.'

'See what I mean?' Martin cried

triumphantly, 'We don't know *who's* in there with him.'

'God, it's his daughter! Alice,' Amber cried. 'I know her slightly. Not that she's allowed out much. Oh Christ, what's she done to deserve that?'

'What did our parents do?' Roger asked rhetorically.

'But his daughter. Can't we help her?' Amber wondered while the boys shook their heads.

'Not a chance. Face the Korean? In your dreams. Look, there they go.' He indicated where Kalo, driving the car, was disappearing out of sight.

'She's so pretty. That night at the ball, she looked gorgeous—' Amber was saying.

'—in that beaded dress,' Roger agreed. 'She was the one with Rudi Wolfe.'

'Yes. You know him?'

Martin frowned. 'I know *of* him. Rudolph Wolfe,' he mused. 'He writes for *Newsdesk.* I've read him. He's good. Sharp.' He looked at Roger. 'Do you think he might . . . ?'

Roger shrugged, catching his drift. 'Maybe. I was, no, *we* were there the night Jonathan Crawley introduced him to the group. He said he was working. Or so I got the impression.'

'Yes. Like, we were in *Vesuvio*,' Amber interrupted. 'Eating pizza. Jonathan hailed him over—'

'What was he doing in Juan les Pins? What's

there to write about there? For a man like Rudi Wolfe?'

Amber shrugged. 'On holiday?' she speculated.

Roger shook his head. 'No. He's not the type. And he *said.* The way he was dressed . . .'

'Like me when I first got here?' Martin offered and Amber snorted, '*Not* like you! Much classier. But I agree. Smart shirts, dark chinos. Not holiday clothes. Besides, his *attitude* wasn't holiday.' Then she added, 'And his skin was the whitest I'd ever seen.'

'Then do you suppose he was writing an article on Victor Sandar?' Martin said, stating what as in all their minds.

'Yeah! Everyone is interested in that gangster,' Roger said in disgust. 'Dying to read about him. Rehash his dirty scandalous past. Slobbering over the gory details. Why the hell are people so avid to read about the lives of villians?'

'Maybe he was just using Alice to get to the bastard,' Amber hazarded.

'No. He really looked smitten that night at the ball,' Martin countered, remembering the couple, the way they looked at each other. 'I wonder. Maybe he really fell for her.'

'Sure. What a dilemma. If it's true. Mind you he was up that tree for ages.'

'Well, does it matter?' Martin enquired. 'If he just wants a story on Sandar, or he loves the daughter, who cares? He's got an interest in

199

the Sandar family and I think we should tell him about what we saw.'

Roger looked doubtful. 'How's that going to help us with Sandar?' he asked.

Martin sighed again. 'Look. Victor Sandar is not going to walk out of that house again. He's not going to put as much as the tip of his nose outside. Not going to take any chances. Not after the shooting. He's paranoid anyway. You've only got to check out security, like I did. He's not going to just take a stroll, believe me,' he explained patiently. 'And I'm not going to send in poisoned wine or blow up the place, so you can discard those ideas. I've no intention of spending my life in prison. I feel my family has suffered enough and if I get caught—'

'*We* get caught,' Roger interpolated.

'*We* get caught going in like Kamikaze pilots and have to go to prison or, like, blow ourselves up like those freedom fighters, I'm not your man. I definitely don't want to be a martyr. The whole operation would be wasted and Victor Sandar will have won again.'

'He's right, Roger,' Amber agreed. 'We can't afford to take too many chances.'

'Thing is,' Martin said, 'it's not going to do us any harm to tell Rudolph Wolfe what we saw. Just what we *saw*, not what we're planning.'

They agreed, deciding to get to Rudi and think about what further action they might take when they sussed out the lie of the land.

'There's a gardener who drinks in the café in the port,' Martin said. 'I can try to find out from him what happened in the Sandar villa behind closed doors. It's amazing what the staff get to know.'

They left the little house and went down to the port in Antibes and sat at a table on the pavement in the market and drank espresso. Crowds milled about idly, window shopping, picking up necklaces or earrings, trying them on or draping the hand-painted shawls around their shoulders, examining paintings reminiscent of other more famous artists or copies of Monet, Matisse or Van Gogh, wondering if they could get away with pretending they were originals. There were a lot of painters using dots. A few old men with tobacco-stained moustaches played checkers and others, in the opening of the little stalls, watched the world go by.

Martin felt he fitted in much better now, in his new persona. Casually, elegantly clothed and with his hair bleached, his manners had automatically changed and he had become more authoritative. He found himself assuming leadership where before he had been reluctant, and he had felt vaguely disadvantaged. He had been able to put paid very firmly to the worst excesses and bizarre plans put forward by Amber and her brother.

'Where can we find him?' he asked now.

'Rudi.'

'Jonathan would know,' Amber said eagerly.

'Well, phone him. Just ask for the number though. Don't tell him *anything.*' Martin did not trust them to be discreet.

'I got to see Baba man,' Amber said suddenly rising, hurrying away and disappearing around a corner between two stalls. They waited patiently. Martin did not ask where she had gone. They chatted in a desultory way about nothing in particular. When she reappeared about ten minutes later she seemed calmer but anxious to leave the area.

Roger drove them in her car up the boulevard to the Crawleys' villa. Jonathan was, as it happened, out somewhere. 'Probably playing tennis with the Fontaines,' Roger guessed.

They asked Terry, the houseboy at the villa, where Jonathan was and Roger's guess proved correct.

'I don't suppose you'd have Monsieur Rudolph Wolfe's telephone number?' Amber enquired.

Terry gave them a huge smile and said yes, he could give them Monsieur Wolfe's number.

'All the numbers are on the wall,' he told them, leading them into the kitchen where the chef was labouring over preparations for a lobster lunch, boiling the struggling *crusti* for a Thermidor.

There was a telephone database that ran into ten or twelve pages and on it were listed the names of regulars and provisioners in the vicinity in alphabetical order.

'Guests here, in the South of France,' Terry explained, delighted at the extent of his knowledge, thrilled to be of help. 'There, friends in London, New York.' He spread his hands. 'On computer is all their friends. Here current ones. Their tastes, their allergies, their likes and dislikes. Food they can eat, food they can't.' He grinned even wider. 'Like nuts. Some can't have nuts. Some can't have dairy. Some on a diet. Lots of people don' like fat. Me, I love it.'

Amber stared with thinly disguised envy at the servant's slim compact body. 'You'll live to regret it. You'll end up gross.' But the boy shook his head.

'No. My Pa eats the same I do. So does my uncle. They like me.' He patted his firm flat belly. 'Runs in the family,' he said.

Martin was flicking through the address list to the W's.

'Got it,' he cried triumphantly. Then he turned to the grinning houseboy, 'Thank you so much. Appreciate your help.'

'You wanna use the telephone?' the ever helpful Terry asked. 'One on the terrace outside.'

He led them to the loungers outside the open French windows where there was a phone on an occasional table.

Martin was very surprised to find Rudi in. He sounded breathless and explained he'd just walked in, gone to his room and they'd called him back down again.

'I'm at the top of the house,' he laughed.

'You tied up with Alice Sandar?' Martin cut to the chase.

'Yes. Yes, why?' Rudi's voice was filled with alarm. Martin explained.

'Oh God, oh God. Where are you?'

'At the Crawleys'.'

'I'm coming over.'

'No. Let me try to find out where they've gone first. I know one of the Sandar staff. He drinks—' But the phone had gone dead.

\*　　　\*　　　\*

Rudi arrived and although his manner was calm they could see the tension around his mouth and the wildness in his eyes.

'I've got to try to get to speak to Alice's mother,' he told them. 'She's sympathetic.'

'But how? He'll not let you near her.' They all knew who Roger meant.

They sat silently staring out over the summer scene, the glorious panorama before them. The bay sparkled in the sunshine and the waves danced gleefully sending off diamond shafts of light and washing the villa in a reflected silver sheen. Rudi paced the terrace

204

ignoring the drinks Terry brought them. He stopped suddenly and clicked his fingers.

'I know. I've got it,' he cried. 'Come on.'

He had remembered Nola Reine, the Comtesse de Sevigné. He knew she would help and she was the only one at the moment who knew how Victor Sandar thought.

He left the others at a café-bar while he went to talk to her. He told Martin, meantime, to check out the gardener.

'I don't think he'll be able to help, though,' he told Martin. 'Victor Sandar is not going to tell anyone where he's sent his daughter.'

He was furious. Anger raged through him threatening to overwhelm him. Rage such as he had never felt before made him grip the wheel of the car till his knuckles were white.

If Victor had harmed her! Oh God, his mind screamed, don't let him have harmed her, my love, my darling. He very nearly ran into the Pontiac in front. The driver shook a fist out of the window and made an obscene gesture and Rudi pulled himself together. He'd be of no use to Alice in a police station.

Nola Reine lived in a large apartment in Nice and was looked after by an elderly black-uniformed dame with a hatchet face, a sour manner and a heart as big as the Sahara. The apartment was oppressively grand and darkly sombre on this bright day. The walls were wine-coloured and covered top to bottom with paintings and photographs of Nola Reine in her glamorous heyday. Heavy velvet curtains covered the floor-to-ceiling windows and the whole atmosphere was gloomy, hot and musty.

The hatchet-faced woman who treated Rudi as if he were Jack the Ripper went reluctantly to fetch her mistress and shortly thereafter wheeled Nola in. She looked very old and dejected but when she saw who it was she brightened up.

'Dearest boy! What a sight for sore eyes. Wonderful to see you again.'

'I hope I don't intrude,' Rudi said politely, his impatience barely concealed.

'No, no, of course not. I only wish I had more intrusions. Please sit down. Hannah, bring us some tea.' She looked back at Rudi. 'Unless you would prefer something stronger?' Rudi shook his head and the woman left, having looked him up and down with a belligerent eye that seemed to warn him to be kind to her mistress. Rudi returned her glare with a reassuring nod.

'You are such a pleasure to look at, Rudi Wolfe, that I welcome any intrusion you might make.' She laughed and as he sat on the sofa she continued, 'But sadly you did not come here to flirt with me, dear boy, now did you?' Rudi shook his head. 'So what can I do for you? There is anguish in your eyes and that kind of agony is reserved for one's lover. Alice? Am I right?' She took his hand and held it. He was trembling and he squeezed her fingers so hard that tears came into her eyes.

He explained the situation. Nola nodded.

'It is Victor Sandar all over,' she said. 'Typical of him. Oh, Rudi, he's not a man to take on lightly, I did warn you.'

'I love her. It's no good telling me—'

'That much?'

He looked at Nola with level, burning eyes. 'That much,' he said defiantly. She nodded, sighing.

'Oh well! If it's that much, honey, there's no hope for you.'

'She needs my help,' he said softly.

'I think you'd help any girl in her position,' Nola mused. 'But Alice . . . ah, you've become a real Sir Lancelot.'

'Yes. I'd die for her,' he told Nola fervently.

'So, what can I do?' she asked brightly. 'I'm not exactly Sir Lancelot or Sir Tristan, riding to the rescue, now am I? I can't see myself doing a James Bond, can you?'

'All you've got to do,' he told her eagerly, 'is make a phone call.'

'Oh!' She blinked rapidly. 'Do tell.'

'Yes. Invite Cynthia Sandar over. She's on our side, I know she is. She'll help. We've just got to get her out of the house.'

'Of course!' Nola exclaimed. 'He won't suspect anything. He doesn't know who the Comtesse de Sevigné is, only that she is a titled friend and therefore above suspicion. Oh, the folly of social climbers!'

She pushed her wheelchair to the table and picked up the phone.

'You're not just a pretty face,' she told Rudi as she dialled the number. 'But I still don't hold out much hope for you.'

## CHAPTER TWENTY-TWO

'Kalo, I need to go to the bathroom.'

She spoke gently, keeping her voice level as if it was an everyday occurrence for her to be kidnapped from her own home.

'You have to hold on.' His eyes were on the road before them as he drove.

They had driven in silence to Genoa, through the tunnels and along the coast seeing benign blue sea and sky before plunging into darkness, the glare of lights depriving Alice of vision. After Genoa they had driven north through the valleys for another two hours and now they were crossing the peaceful and fertile farmland continuing north towards Turin where the Alps began.

She'd done screaming and yelling ages ago and had realised that it would get her nowhere. She curled up in silence, her mind busy, trying to find a way to squirrel out of the situation. The only advantage she had was that Kalo had always cared for her. She could not believe for one moment that he would harm her. But she knew that once she was in that place—that clinic—it would be difficult to prove her sanity and there would be little hope of escape.

'Please, Kalo! *Please.* I'm bursting!'

'Okay, okay,' he grumbled. 'But no tricks, mind!'

'You don't have to worry about me, Kalo,' she said in as cheerful a tone as she could manage. 'Daddy's won. He always does. So it's best for me to give in. I've no option, have I?'

Kalo had been in a state of acute anxiety about the trip and on hearing what Alice said he heaved a sigh of relief. His boss was often unreasonable and this undertaking had given him nightmares. He had been ordered to take the screaming struggling girl on a long trip during which they were going to have to cross borders and passport control. How on earth did Mr Sandar expect him to control his daughter at checkpoints if she remained uncooperative? Kalo had been agonizing over these seemingly insurmountable problems when Alice had appeared to fall asleep and silence reigned in the car leaving Kalo to more gloomy speculation.

Then she'd awakened and was docile. Kalo was vastly relieved. Her cooperation was essential for a smooth run to Switzerland. So when she asked for a pit-stop Kalo was relaxed and allowed his charge to get out of the car and use the *Dames* at a gas station on the road.

He even unlocked the handcuffs and let her go by herself to the restroom.

Kalo was not, however, a fool and he had not held down his job because he was stupid. Alice did not underestimate him. He had chosen a filling station in the middle of the countryside. If she made a run for it they both knew it would be dead easy to pick her up. There was no hiding place anywhere, no tree or house, nothing but open road.

Kalo waited in the car to see what she would do.

Alice, knowing Kalo, guessed his motive. She was manipulating him, hoping he would come to trust her. She emerged into the sunlight. She looked at him where he sat in the car, gestured towards the sign advertising Magnum ice-cream and mouthed, 'Can I?' He nodded and she fished out some coins. Having purchased the ice-cream she hurried back to the car licking it greedily.

'God, I was hungry,' she said, getting in. 'Okay, Kalo. On we go!'

Inside she was shaking. Her whole being was alert. True, she was terrified, but like a frightened animal she was on her guard, primed to act. She knew that she must be ready to take a chance when it was offered. She also knew that if Kalo succeeded in getting her into the clinic in Switzerland that she would be lost. If her father made good his promise and had her sectioned then there would be no way out. She'd be shut away with mentally disturbed patients and would probably crack up herself and become as disturbed as they were. She did not think she could remain sane, rational for long under those circumstances. No one could. But she was not going to give in without a fight.

She wanted Rudi. She wanted him so badly it hurt. But she pushed the thought of him away. It was painful, too agonising. Rudi didn't know where she was. Her mother didn't know where she was. How could they find her? Rescue her? No, it was up to her to try to escape.

She shivered, thinking of her father as the car rolled onwards. How could he be so cruel? The shock of his behaviour left her bewildered. Seeing the kindly face of someone you love changing into a mask of hatred and malice was indeed shocking. Jekyll and Hyde. Oh, it was heartbreaking.

She had grown up of a sudden. Been precipitated into adulthood and disillusionment and pain too quickly, too soon.

But she had Rudi. She loved him passionately with all her might and strength and he loved her and somehow she would get to him, home into his arms and they would be together and she could rest. But not now, not yet.

\*       \*       \*

They were driving through the long tunnel. It seemed to go on for hours. When eventually they emerged into the light of day she looked at her watch and an hour had passed.

'Hungry, Kalo?' she hazarded in a light enquiring tone. 'You see somewhere we could stop?' She did not sound too eager, too anxious. Offhand, as if she thought they were out for a casual Sunday jaunt.

'I s'pose,' he agreed reluctantly.

'I had no breakfast,' she pouted. 'Only the Magnum.'

'We'll stop at the next *relais*,' he said and glanced over his shoulder. She stared back at him innocently.

'You needn't worry about me, Kalo. I have no friends. You know that. Daddy never let me.'

He knew that to be true. Very few were brave enough to be friends with the gangster's daughter. How could you side against such a man as Alice's father was?

'You not give me no trouble?'

She shook her head. 'No. I promise.'

It would be a waste of time. She had thought for a wild moment of protesting at Passport Control but had jettisoned the idea. Kalo had mentioned that he had doctor's certificates saying she was unstable.

'This okay?' he asked gruffly. They had stopped at a roadhouse offering food and

212

drink, a quaint isolated place that Kalo felt confident about.

She waited for him while he locked the car, then in her sunniest voice she cried, 'Lunch, Kalo. Gosh, I'm starving!' And together they entered the hotel.

# CHAPTER TWENTY-THREE

Cynthia accepted Nola Reine's invitation to lunch that day. Nola referred to herself as the Comtesse and a sixth sense told Cynthia that it had something to do with Alice. She could not think how or why but some instinct told her this was not merely a social invitation. There was also the fact that she only knew Nola slightly and had never cultivated her nor been cultivated by her. And Nola had said, 'Tell your husband that the Comtesse de Sevigné wants to get to know you better.'

In any event, Cynthia was prepared to clutch at any straw, however remote, that promised a solution.

It turned out that her instinct was right.

She had not seen Victor since the morning. Her husband had locked himself into his study and she had spent the time groping for some way out of the mess. And then, out of the blue, the call came from Nola, a woman she hardly knew.

'Tell my husband, if he asks, that I'm having lunch with the Comtesse de Sevigné,' she told Nana and left the villa.

She was delighted to find Rudi Wolfe with the erstwhile star. And relieved. She had not realised how helpless she had felt and how desperately she craved support and understanding until that moment. And she trusted Rudi. There was something very dependable about him and she turned to him now in trustful supplication.

'You'll rescue her?' she asked and he nodded eagerly.

'It's crazy,' she whispered through tears of relief. 'We're talking as if we were in a novel by Baroness Orczy!'

*The Scarlet Pimpernel?*' He smiled at her. 'But I can do nothing until I know where she's been taken.'

'Switzerland. To a clinic. He intends to section her.'

Rudi, who had been standing in the dark room, sat down abruptly and, sickened at the thought, shook his head.

Nola cried, '*Mon Dieu*! The devil!'

'You don't know what he can be like,' Cynthia whispered.

Nola shook her head, 'Oh yes I do,' she muttered.

She rang for Hannah and when the woman entered she ordered tea and sandwiches for them all. Hannah growled something and left.

214

Nola shrugged. 'Poor woman!' she remarked, referring to the servant. She straightened her wine-coloured velvet turban. 'It's an invasion! We have not had so many people here in a long time. Anything more elaborate than sandwiches would be straining her culinary ability. I usually have soup and salad on a tray. So the poor old dear is feeling demented and put-upon.'

'We don't need food, really we don't,' Cynthia protested.

'Oh yes you do,' Nola insisted. 'People in a crisis always refuse food and it is the one thing they really *do* need. And you don't know when you'll get the chance again. Besides, it will do her good. Show her how spoiled she is. She needs to bestir herself from time to time.' She looked at her visitors who were pacing the floor in different directions.

'Sit down please, both of you. You're making me dizzy,' she ordered. 'How can we sort this mess out unless we compose ourselves?'

Neither Cynthia nor Rudi had any idea where Victor had banished his daughter and until Nola interrupted their anxious speculations their ideas bordered on the excessive.

'We could phone the Embassy, send out an SOS,' Cynthia suggested.

'No. The police. We'll telephone the police in Zurich and Geneva.'

'Fax them. We'll fax them—'

'And tell them to send out the Swiss army to rescue a young woman sent there by her father, driven by her chauffeur? Don't be daft!' Nola interrupted.

'Have you got a better suggestion?' Cynthia asked.

'Listen to me,' Nola said. 'Victor Sandar is a creature of habit. He's predictable. I think you'll agree? And he sticks to his friends, the people he trusts, has bought.'

'Yes, but . . .' Cynthia paused, staring at Nola, perplexed.

'How do I know?' The old star smiled. 'That's another story. Rudi will fill you in, Cynthia. So. Once, long ago, he recommended to me—well, he suggested—a hideaway, a place in Switzerland. He said they were 'in his pocket'. It was near Montreux. It's a wild guess, but'—she shrugged—'I think it is the place. Where else would he know?'

Cynthia was frowning. 'I've heard of . . .'— she clicked her fingers as she thought—'. . . *La Piedmonterre*.' She smiled triumphantly. 'One of Victor's henchmen had to disappear. Victor was talking on the phone. He said '*La Piedmonterre*'. I remember. And the man went to Switzerland.'

'So it must be there.'

'But how can we get there before them?' Cynthia asked.

Rudi could feel the panic rising. 'We'll fly to

Geneva,' he said.

'I'm old,' Nola said. 'In my day a train. Nowadays fly, always fly.'

'If I could I'd get Concorde,' Rudi muttered.

'Bring her here, Rudi, when you find her,' Nola instructed him. 'She'll be safe here.'

'Now we must go.' Rudi rose impatiently. 'Come on, Cynthia.'

'Don't you think we should phone the airport?'

Rudi shook his head. 'No. I think we need to be there in person, bribe if necessary, get someone to swop. No, we need to be there.'

It was an extremely disgruntled Hannah who, on bringing in the carefully prepared sandwiches was met by a room empty of visitors and only her mistress dozing in her chair.

## CHAPTER TWENTY-FOUR

They reached Geneva that evening and booked into a lakeside hotel for the night. Cynthia was too emotionally charged to sleep and she and Rudi dined together quietly in the chandelier-lit hotel restaurant.

'We're working in the dark,' Rudi said. 'It's so damn frustrating. We don't know if she's already incarcerated or what they've done to her.'

'Hush, Rudi. You'll achieve nothing projecting like that. Leave it. We'll sort it, never fear. I am her mother after all. This is one time Victor won't win.' Her face was set and stony. Neither of them ate much.

He told her all about Nola Reine and her affair with Victor. All Cynthia said was a cryptic, 'Typical.' Then she looked at him searchingly.

'You love my daughter very much, don't you, Rudi?' she asked.

'You know I do,' he said quietly. She had only to look into his eyes to know he was telling the truth, to see the strength of his love. She nodded her head, satisfied.

They telephoned *La Piedmonterre* and enquired about a new patient. To Cynthia's surprise the person at the other end was friendly and forthcoming. She had assumed that like in the movies they'd be secretive. They were not and Cynthia realised that they probably did not think there was anything not entirely above board about the booking.

Yes, they were expecting a new patient, a Miss Alice Sandar. She was to arrive in the morning. No, the receptionist had no idea where she was staying but she could say they were on their way from France. Driving.

'What will we do?' Cynthia whispered when she had thanked the girl and rung off. 'Once Kalo delivers her through the gates of that

218

place it is going to be almost impossible to get her out.'

'She'll not get that far,' Rudi promised grimly.

'How can we stop them?' Cynthia asked. 'That car is bullet-proof. No one could get her out of it.'

Rudi looked at her intently. 'How far are you prepared to go?' he asked her.

'As far as I have to,' she told him.

'Good.' His mouth was set. 'No lingering loyalty to Victor?'

She shook her head. 'None,' she said with firm conviction.

'Because I'm involving the police,' Rudi stated firmly. 'Listen, Cynthia. Victor Sandar has got away with so much evil because people *let* him. He hasn't got a friend anywhere. He's got people scared of him is all. They do what he tells them, but they don't like it. So what I propose is this. We talk to the Swiss Polizei. Get them to ring Scotland Yard and the Sûreté if necessary. Fill in the picture. Tell the truth. Your daughter has been forced against her will to leave you and her home. We'll be there to meet Kalo when he arrives at *La Piedmonterre*. The rest is up to your daughter. If Alice tells them the truth they'll have to let her go. Kalo is holding her against her wishes and that's a crime in any country in Europe.'

'Do you think she will? Tell what happened! Or is she still under her father's thumb?'

Cynthia asked him.

'I don't know,' Rudi shrugged. 'I simply don't know.'

The mountains rose piercing the cloudy sky as they drove to the clinic just outside Montreux. Below them the lake sparkled bright blue in the sun. Cute little chalets dotted the hills and the top of the mountains were glimmering snowy pillows. It looked as if they were covered in icing sugar.

It was pleasantly cool after the Côte d'Azur, the green hills peaceful, the cows and sheep placid in the pearly morning light.

Rudi had got in touch with the Swiss police in Geneva after dinner the night before. He told Cynthia he could not sleep.

I won't sleep a wink and I can't wait,' he told her. 'I'll feel better if I get the ball rolling, kick-start the action.' Cynthia agreed. Being patient when a loved one is in danger is not easy.

The Swiss police had been methodical, thorough and open-minded. They had eventually reached the conclusion that the elegant, English lady Cynthia Sandar and the young American journalist—they had phoned the French office of *Newsdesk* to check him out—were in fact telling the truth, that the evil gangster Victor Sandar was indeed going to force his daughter to leave their home and incarcerate her in *La Piedmonterre* against her will and that Alice was one hundred per cent sane.

'We watch that place, Madame,' the Swiss Polizei told Cynthia in Geneva. Lips pursed, he shook his head disapprovingly. 'We do not like what goes on there, the people who come and go, but they have not, so far, broken the rules. They have not transgressed the law. But it is unsavoury.'

'My daughter was handcuffed,' Cynthia told him tearfully. 'She was dragged forcibly out of her home. She will be very distressed.' The worthy Swiss tut-tutted and shook his head.

The Swiss police were able to inform the anxious Cynthia and Rudi that Alice and Kalo had spent the night in a *relais* in Montreux.

'They are not unremarkable,' the Polizei told them. 'A very large Korean and a beautiful young girl. Together.' Cynthia's eyes widened in alarm.

'You don't mean . . . ?'

'No, no! They were in separate rooms. But the concierge I spoke with says the Korean locked the girl in. And the room was on the fourth floor. So he obviously took no chances.'

Cynthia looked relieved at this piece of information.

\*        \*        \*

They wasted no time next morning. Cynthia and Rudi were on their way at the crack of dawn. Both of them were acutely on edge, tension and anxiety building as they neared the clinic.

'Suppose it's not the right clinic?' Cynthia was filled with an awful fear that they were on an entirely wrong trail.

'They said they expected her.'

'Suppose it's a trap?'

'I think we can trust Nola,' Rudi said, but he too felt desperately anxious.

It was an enchanted morning. The sun was a hazy buttercup yellow as they sped along the country lanes, though they neither noticed nor cared about the pretty scenery.

Arriving at the high iron gates they pressed the bell. The gates opened and they rolled up the drive.

The Polizei were there before them. They parked with the other cars and waited.

*     *     *

*La Piedmonterre* looked serene and peaceful in the beautiful morning. Kalo, glancing around, saw the cars parked but they looked normal in the peaceful, hazy dawn. The Polizei cars were unmarked and therefore unnoticeable. He thought nothing of the crowded apron in front of the clinic. Cars these days were parked everywhere. The whole world was a parking lot and Europe was cars wall to wall.

He walked to the intercom beside the iron doors and was about to press the buzzer and

222

speak into it when he felt himself suddenly and firmly thrust against the gates and he was handcuffed neatly and efficiently with no fuss at all. His rights were being read to him by a burly Swiss and Kalo had no time to collect himself. No time to escape or make a run for it. He was trussed up, disarmed, rendered effectively helpless. He looked over his shoulder to see his charge run into her boyfriend's arms and his boss's wife in tears, kissing her daughter, holding her as if she would never let her go. It dawned on him then that it was all over. The game was up. And it had been a trap. He, Kalo, had walked into a trap. Philosophically, he decided his best bet was to go quietly. He'd say he was just obeying orders.

As they led him to one of the cars he shook his head, bemused at how the peaceful Swiss countryside had so suddenly erupted into such activity and at how all Victor Sandar's carefully laid plans had been turned upside down. It had never happened like that before in Kalo's experience. His boss must be slipping. That old chestnut had worked for others, more important than he.

Within a few moments it was all over, the cars purring quietly away leaving the entrance to the clinic deserted. There was one client that would not be checking in that day.

# CHAPTER TWENTY-FIVE

They held on to each other for dear life. Alice was shivering uncontrollably, shock taking its toll. She clung to Rudi as if fearful he might vanish and he soothed her, cradling her in his arms.

'I thought I'd never see you again,' she whispered through chattering teeth.

'Me too,' Rudi said grimly.

The Swiss policeman gave her a flask of brandy to sip from.

'It will calm you,' he told her kindly. He had asked her formally to verify the fact that she was being held against her will. Alice had not hesitated.

'Very much against my will,' she assured them. She gulped the fiery liquid greedily.

'Kalo didn't hurt you?' Cynthia asked. Alice shook her head.

'No, Mummy.' She shivered. 'I'm not going back there, am I Mummy? Daddy can't force me, can he?'

'No, of course not.'

'And I'm not going home. I never want to go there again.'

'No, my dearest. And I'm not either. Do what he will, I'll not stay with Victor a moment longer.'

'Then where are you taking me?' Alice

asked anxiously.

'We're going to get the plane to Nice and then we're going to stay with the Comtesse de Sevigné. Nola Reine,' Rudi told her. 'She'll look after you.'

'Will we be safe?'

'He'll never hurt you, dearest,' Cynthia told her. 'He'll probably kill me eventually, but I'll never go back to him.'

Alice broke away from her love and turned to her mother. 'Oh Mummy, he can't! He couldn't! He wouldn't kill you, surely?'

'I'm afraid you don't know your father very well. Leaving him is my death sentence.'

'Then the police would arrest him,' Alice argued. 'And he'd never risk that.'

'Oh, he'll not kill me himself, Alice. He'll get some minion—the hired help—to execute me.'

'Oh Mummy, don't say that,' Alice pleaded. 'I couldn't bear it. Maybe if I saw Daddy—Father—pleaded with him—'

'You'll do no such thing,' Rudi protested, aghast. 'Good grief, girl, after what he has done to you, don't you see how dangerous he is?'

'It wouldn't do any good, pet,' Cynthia told her. 'He'd give you his word, promise you whatever you asked and then I'd be found over a cliff full of pills or heroin or whisky. Something like that. And he'd have a cast-iron alibi. Lots of witnesses.' She shrugged. 'The thing is, Alice, when you don't care what people think, you win. And when you are determined to kill someone, you can. All it takes is time and patience and well-paid employees who are aware that if they screw up or grass they and their family are dead. Victor Sandar has all that and more.' Cynthia shook her head sadly, then looked at Rudi. 'You'll look after her, Rudi, won't you?' she asked. He read the anxiety in her eyes. If Cynthia's life was threatened, so was Alice's. He nodded.

'I'll take her to America. Boston. New York. I don't think Victor Sandar's arm reaches that far.' But Cynthia did not seem convinced.

They did not reach Nola until evening. The sun was a glowing flame-coloured disc on the edge of a black velvet sea when they finally arrived at her apartment.

Hannah showed them into the huge drawing-room where, in candle light, the many glamorous faces of the star stared down at them from the walls, ghosts from another era. On the table the sandwiches Hannah had made for them before they left sat expectantly under their clingfilm wrap. She parked the travellers there, triumphantly peeled the clingfilm off the plates and went to get her mistress.

They fell on the food hungrily. By the time she returned, wheeling Nola in, the sandwiches were all gone. She gave a satisfied smile as she kicked the brake down on Nola's wheelchair and left them.

'You are welcome,' Nola greeted them and when Rudi kissed her cheek she patted his hand, tears in her eyes. 'I'm so relieved to see you. You must tell me all. Relax now. You are safe here. Hannah has instructions to let no one in, and,' she grinned at them, 'as you have polished off her sandwiches she will be pleased. Victor won't expect you to come here, will he?'

Cynthia shook her head in agreement. 'You're very kind, Contessa,' she told her hostess a trifle tearfully. 'Have you heard anything? From the villa?'

'All is silence,' Nola replied. 'But I wouldn't hear, would I? Poor Victor can hardly admit to the world his true position regarding his wife and child. In the immortal words of Oscar Wilde, "To lose a wife is unfortunate, to lose a daughter as well is carelessness"! Of course I've paraphrased. Now relax. Don't worry about Victor.'

But Cynthia could not forget him. She knew him too well not to be very anxious. And he'd find out. Kalo would phone him. He'd be insanely angry that Alice had escaped, shaken with furious rage because his womenfolk had dared to disobey him. There would be no reasoning with him; it would be a fool who would approach Victor Sandar at this moment in time and an idiot who would underestimate his danger.

When Alice and Cynthia had retired Nola spoke to Rudi.

'I was lying,' she said. 'He telephoned here after you'd gone.'

They sat in front of her small fire. Cynthia and Alice had gone to sleep in the larger guestroom while Rudi was allocated a small spare bedroom at the rear of the apartment beside Hannah's room and the kitchen.

'You'll have to curb your ardour.' Nola grinned evilly at Rudi who gave her a wan smile.

'I just want to hold her,' he said. 'Just keep reassuring myself she's safe.'

'Tonight she'll rest in her mother's arms,' Nola told him.

They sat on either side of the fire and talked. It was stifling in the room, airless and musty but Rudi was thankful to be there.

'I often complained of how dull life was,' Nola told Rudi. 'Missed the old days.' She gestured briefly to the glamour stills on the wall. 'But the drama we've had here the last few days takes some beating. I've loved it.' she added mischievously. 'People crying, hysterics, tantrum, rushing about, running away, clandestine meetings. It makes some people ill, I know, but not me. I thrive on it all. It's the flavour of life for me.' She sighed. 'I've felt dead for a long time and then you came along, Rudi. Everything perked up.' She smiled at him now, a little sadly. 'But to tell the truth,

Rudi, it's worn me out.'

'Nola, you're tired. You must rest. *I* must rest.'

But they both seemed reluctant to leave the fireside. While they lingered Nola told him about Victor's call.

'I didn't want to worry Cynthia or Alice,' she said. 'You see, he threatened. He'd guessed where you were.'

'What did he say?' Rudi asked, his eyes narrowed.

'Well, he phoned and I pretended I didn't know what he was talking about. He said, "Cynthia said she was meeting you for lunch. I want to know what time to expect her." Very casual he was. I said, "Nonsense. You must have heard wrong." He said, very coldly, "No. I did not." I said, "I very rarely go out of the house. You know I'm in a wheelchair. You saw me at the Crawleys' dinner. And I'm afraid I haven't seen your wife." I knew he didn't believe me. He said, "If you're hiding her you'll regret it. And you'll pay for it." His tone sent shivers down my back, Rudi. I spoiled everything then. I said, "I've heard that before, Victor. It has no effect on me any more." I could hear him gasp. I'd jogged his memory which was unwise, though I'm sure he still doesn't recognise me or guess who I am. Or was. The Comtesse de Sevigné is a long way from Nola Reine.' She smiled at him, a naughty glint in her eyes. 'At my age what can he do? Kill me is all and as I'm due to fall off the perch any day now, what do I care? No, Rudi, each day is a bonus. But'—she wagged her finger at Rudi—'I care very much what happens to you and Alice. And, strangely enough, I care what happens to Cynthia. She's a true blue-blood. Not like me. I married it but she was born a lady and she has been through hell. I'd like to see her meet a decent guy who'd love her and look after her. Make up for the past. And you,'—she sighed—'Rudi, you are a beautiful young man. You must have children. Oh, to be young again.' She glanced at the pictures on the walls. 'You think Alice Sandar would stand a chance with you if I was that girl again? I tell you no! You'd be mine. I'd vamp you into submission and you would be enslaved.'

He smiled at her, not contradicting her. She went on, 'But see, I'm old and tired and what I want for you is a long peaceful life with your Alice. So you take care.'

He nodded. 'I will. I promise.'

'Now, Rudi, ring for Hannah and off you go to bed.' And she waved her hand in dismissal.

After he'd gone Nola steered the wheelchair to her bedroom and opened the top drawer of her bureau. The gun lay there, shiny steel waiting to be used. On whom?

Her husband the Comte had bought it long, long ago for her protection. There had been a spate of break-ins along the Côte d'Azur and he, anxious and loving man that he was, had insisted she have the weapon for her protection. She had put it in the bureau drawer and more or less forgotten it. It lay there now, loaded, ready for use and she stared at it, a rueful smile on her lips.

Nola felt very tired. She had enjoyed the excitement of the past week. It had energised her, given her an interest in a life that had become dull and monotonous. She had vegetated for a long time and events had reminded her of a time when romance happened, adventures happened, *life* happened. But that was a long time ago and now she realised that she did not want adventure any longer. That time for her, that feeling of aliveness was over. It was no longer enjoyable.

Also she did not want to indulge in nostalgia any longer. The past needed to be buried. It held no magic for her. And it was frightening that she could no longer visualise a future.

It had been a good life, except for the fact that she had no children, she had no regrets. And that had been Victor Sandar's fault. Damn him. He had poisoned the lives of everyone he came into contact with. She knew he would not let his wife and daughter go just like that.

So she took out the gun and put it under her pillow. It would live there during the night and under the rug on her knees during the day. If

Victor sent someone she'd be ready. This was one battle Victor Sandar was not going to win.

Hannah came and helped her into bed and she lay there for a long time, thinking. Her thoughts depressed her.

Victor Sandar would not give up. They were fools if they imagined he would. She thought of the others sleeping peacefully all around her in the apartment, imagining everything would turn out all right. The optimism of youth.

They'd have to work out a plan of action tomorrow after breakfast. They'd have to act quickly if they were to thwart Victor Sandar.

She picked up her Bible and turned the pages until the book fell open at the eleventh psalm. She began to read.

'See the wicked bracing their bow;
they are fixing their arrows on the string
to ambush the upright by stealth . . .' and,
  at last,
'The Lord is just and loves justice;
the upright shall see his face.'

Rudi and Alice slept deeply that night. Only Cynthia lay awake, afraid to move lest she disturb her daughter curled up deep in sleep beside her.

Cynthia, like Nola, was sure Victor would make a decisive move. His fierce egotistical pride would not permit him to allow her to escape his clutches. She and Alice were his possessions and he would never tolerate their escape from him. The two of them belonged to him and must be caught and returned.

As the minutes ticked by Cynthia speculated, uselessly, she knew, about how he would accomplish this. Knowing, acknowledging for the first time how savage he could be, how utterly ruthless, she too prayed fervently that a loving God would protect her daughter.


## CHAPTER TWENTY-SIX

Victor Sandar sat in his study in the *Villa Bella Vista* chewing his bottom lip and trying to think clearly.

It had all gone wrong, terribly wrong, yet he could not see what he could have done to prevent the mess he now found himself in and try as he might he could not fathom how it had happened.

Kalo was in a Swiss jail. The fact infuriated him. It was an appalling affront to his status. He was lost without his stalwart aide. He had not realised how he depended on the Korean. Manny was Cynthia's servant as was Nana and shouting at them had got him absolutely nowhere; Manny, the cook, was at the moment sitting at the table in the kitchen completely undone, weeping, and Nana had locked herself into Alice's room and refused to come out. As for his wife and child, the possibility that they would leave him had never occurred to him. Such an event was unthinkable, could not possibly happen.

But it had, and Victor was beside himself, overcome with impotent rage, his ego badly dented, his pride damaged. Waves of fury engulfed him.

He could not keep hold of his thoughts long enough to form a plan, decide what action to take. Outrage fragmented his ability to think clearly and he fumed and fretted and boiled over to no avail, floundering helplessly in a morass of emotions he could not control.

They must be brought back. That much was clear. If Eddie the Ferret heard his wife had pissed off, his daughter had gone, he'd laugh. The big man lost it!

But how? Kalo should be here to deal with it.

Eddie the Ferret was in London and Victor's phone call had sent him to Heathrow to get the first plane to Nice. But all the planes were full and the check-in staff and booking clerks were not impressed by Eddie's attitude or his lurid protestations of a grandmother dying in Nice. He called Victor every hour to let him know the position which only wound his boss up even tighter.

So Victor, stewing in his anger, decided,

completely out of character, to leave the villa, go to the Comtesse de Sevigné and try to prise out of her the whereabouts of his wife and daughter.

He was certain she knew where they were. He would use charm, bribery and at the last resort force if necessary. She was a helpless old biddy ready for the scrap heap so it shouldn't be difficult to scare the living daylights out of her. It was not done in the East End of London, but after all, this was France.

Pleased that he'd reached a decision, that at last he could take action, *do* something, he showered, put on chinos, a Brooks Bros button-down shirt, a blue and white striped seersucker jacket and tan loafers and, feeling smart and together, he did something he'd sworn he'd never do. He left the villa alone.

It was weird leaving the house, getting into the Lexus and driving out into the world by himself. He hadn't driven for years. That had been Kalo's job. To his horror he found he was nervous. Almost frightened. Scared. He couldn't manage the car; his driving was erratic, to say the least. He was terribly unsure of the mechanics of the car, angry that he was ignorant. He could hear the voices—*Victor Sandar can't drive, Victor Sandar can't drive.* One or two near collisions alarmed him so much that he drew into the curb and sat there shaking, whether with fear or rage he did not know.

He would have to get a hold on himself or he would be arrested for some minor driving offence. Wouldn't the police and the media have a field day about that?! They'd kill themselves laughing. The great Victor Sandar, arrested for driving incompetently.

And who knew, once the police got him, what excuses they would make to keep him inside? He was under no illusion as to how the European police felt about him. From Geneva to Naples, from Paris to Madrid, from London to Amsterdam, the law would be only too delighted to lock up Victor Sandar and throw away the key on any pretext at all.

He sat in the car at the sidewalk and looked at the address on the piece of paper in his hand. Nice. He better get going.

It had been easy to get her address. The Comtesse de Sevigné, an aristocratic old biddy. But she had an American accent. Probably a social climber who married the Comte for his title. He frowned. It was vaguely familiar, that voice. He'd hardly noticed her at the Crawleys' party. He'd had to listen to Brompton Crawley's inane ramblings. She'd been in a wheelchair, he remembered that. So much the better for him. Made her more vulnerable.

But if he wanted to get there in one piece he'd have to be careful. Concentrate. Keep his mind on what he was doing, not dwell furiously on what the women in his life had done to him. He thought for a moment about getting a taxi, then discarded the idea as too dangerous. If he had to get away in a hurry . . . no, best go as carefully as possible, take his time.

He was so busy concentrating on driving the Lexus that he did not notice the little Citroën that stuck to his rear all the way to Nice.

*      *      *

Martin had been totally taken aback when, peering out of the guesthouse window, he had spotted Victor, groomed and dapper, leaving the villa, hesitating a while, then getting in the Lexus and driving away.

It had been Martin's turn to keep watch. Amber lay stoned out of her mind in the bed and her brother was sleeping off a hangover in the other room.

Truth to tell, it had been Martin who kept watch most of the night, as well as this morning. He did not disturb them when he saw Victor. He did not want them muddling things for him so he tiptoed quietly out of the place and took Roger's car, sending up a prayer of thanks that the brother and sister always left their keys in the ignition. 'No one would want to steal our cars, they're too tacky,' they said.

Were it not for the fact that Victor was having trouble handling the car, Martin would not have caught him or been able to tail him. But Victor was starting and stopping, the car jerking to and fro like a bucking bronco,

237

Victor Sandar driving the car as if he had an L-plate. Martin found it easy to catch him and tail him.

The Lexus finally shuddered to a halt outside a tall elegant Italian-style apartment building in Nice. To Martin's amazement, Victor Sandar got out of it by himself and, without bodyguards, went to the entrance and rang the bell.

Martin was in a quandary. He had no experience of this sort of thing and was unsure what to do next. Amber had stolen a gun; from where he neither knew nor cared. He tapped it now, reassuring himself it was still in his pocket.

What to do next? He did not think it would be a good idea to ring the bells himself without having a clue who he was looking for. He did not want to find himself refused entrance. Perhaps he could pretend he was delivering something. But what?

He noticed a flower shop on the corner of the street and he crossed the road and bought a bouquet of pretty pink roses and freesia. As he emerged he saw a thick-set woman in black with a large white apron tied round her non-existent waist at the door of the house Victor Sandar had disappeared into. The woman's arms were full; she was carrying bags of groceries and was awkwardly trying to get the key into the door.

He hurried over. 'Allow me, Madame,' he

cried and taking the keys from her he opened the door. The woman blushed and stammered her thanks. As they stepped inside she dropped a bag of tangerines which fell, rolling about the floor.

'Let me help, please.' Martin bent down, retrieving the fruit. 'I'll carry them for you,' he told her, juggling the tangerines.

'No, no, I'll manage,' she cried, but it was obvious she could not. It was the perennial lazy-man's-load.

She took him through a hall to the back of the house, led him up a narrow flight of stairs and through a door into a sun-filled kitchen.

'Put them there,' the woman told him pointing to the kitchen table. He obeyed. She noticed the flowers then and raised her eyebrows.

'Are they for Madame?' she enquired. He nodded, improvising.

'Oh, *Mon Dieu*! It is a long time since the Contessa got flowers from an admirer.' The woman rolled her eyes. '*Ooh la la*. She will be enchanted.'

She opened the outer door in the kitchen which Martin saw led directly into the breakfast room. He could see Alice and Cynthia Sandar sitting peacefully there at the table with Rudi Wolfe and a wizened old lady in a wheelchair.

'Flowers for the Comtesse,' the servant beside him said, but Martin had pushed past her into the room.

Everything happened very quickly after that. Martin was about to warn them that Victor was in the building when the gangster himself burst into the room, his face wild. Pandemonium broke out. Victor was shouting, ordering Cynthia and Alice downstairs to the car, screaming at them red-faced. He yanked Alice to her feet and began to drag her, sobbing and pleading, to the door while Rudi tackled him, trying in the small space to force his arms behind him, doing everything in his power to separate him from Alice without hurting her. It was chaos. Dishes clattered to the ground in the activity. Hannah screamed over and over. The Comtesse ordered them all in loud tones to calm down and discuss this situation calmly. In the midst of this Martin took his gun out. He aimed at the struggling Victor and Rudi and pulled the trigger. There was the deafening sound of the explosion and Rudi fell to the floor.

'Oh God, oh God, oh God!' Alice cried out. Her father let her go for a moment, transfixed at the sight of Rudi on the ground. Alice dropped to her knees, weeping, and bent over her fallen lover.

Victor stood a moment frozen in shock, then turned to see who had fired the shot. To his horror he realised the gun was in the hands of someone he had never seen before but who was familiar. A face from the past, from

London. A ghost from long, long ago, from his violent days, a man he had killed, risen from the dead.

He remembered the scene well. The man's stubborn refusal to pay protection, to toe the line. The blood everywhere. That was the old days, long ago, cops, robbers, power struggles and protection, his struggle for power and his winning it. Grantly Sloane refusing to pay, death and violence.

Victor had been able to prove he had been somewhere else. In a casino on the Edgware Road. That's where witnesses swore he'd been when Grantly Sloane died.

Yet there was Grantly standing before him, a gun in his hand. Only he looked younger, fitter. He was pointing the gun at him. Victor Sandar.

The hand holding the gun shook. Martin had shot the wrong man. Victor understood that instantly. He relaxed. He began to speak when the wiry little woman, ancient as a Chinese sage, stretched up and snatched the gun from him and Victor breathed a sigh of relief.

But the woman said very clearly, very firmly, 'No. Let me do it.' She fired the gun directly at Victor as he dived to the floor, falling over the prone body of Rudi Wolfe. She fired again, accurately. Horribly accurately.

He wondered why. What had he ever done to the Comtesse de Sevigné that her eyes were

241

filled with such hate and loathing? Why should he enrage her so much that she could shoot him like this in cold blood?

She had not hesitated. It was calmly, deliberately done. He realised as he lay there, his blood oozing from him, his daughter crooning over the journalist who lay on the floor beside him that they'd lie. They'd lie about the whole scene. Cynthia, his wife, Alice, his daughter, they'd back her, the Comtesse, get her off. Say it was an accident. Make up some story. He knew that as certainly as he knew he was going to die. The jig was up. He was filled with fear at the realisation and panic made him clench his teeth and stare up at the woman in the wheelchair, his eyes pleading for mercy. But there was no spark of sympathy in the blue stare that met his gaze.

Suddenly his eyes caught sight of an old photograph on the wall of the drawing-room. Lying as he was on the floor he could just see it and he recognised those eyes. They had gazed at him once with passion. And with pain.

Nola Reine. Long, long ago. Nola, the film star who'd loved him, from whom he'd run when the going got tough. And now she looked at him without pity as he lay dying on the floor.

Where had they come from, these demons from the past? What were they doing in this sun-filled kitchen in Nice? The questions were never answered. Victor Sandar gave a

242

convulsive shudder and died.

## CHAPTER TWENTY-SEVEN

Victor Sandar was correct in his assumption. Nola Reine was found innocent of any wrongdoing. Officials in many countries were so infinitely relieved that Victor Sandar was dead that they had to restrain themselves from actually congratulating her.

Her case was airtight. There were witnesses to the accidental shooting. Scotland Yard, the Sûreté, even Mossad and particularly DC Beresford heaved a sigh of relief that the villain had been 'taken out'. Good luck to whoever had pulled the trigger.

In London Eddie the Ferret dived for cover but the police ran him to ground. They banged him up and laid a list of felonies, misdemeanors and GBH allegations against him as long as his arm. And Eddie the Ferret sang. It was all at the instigation of Victor Sandar. Eddie the Ferret thought he was doing a deal, only the police broke their word and he ended up inside doing ten to fifteen. They then proceeded to arrest the names he had given them and that was that. Victor Sandar's reign was well and truly over.

Under French law Nola was guilty until proved innocent but the case, public sympathy, the French love of *crimes passionnels* (her love affair with the dead man all came out), the *gendarmes* bending over backwards to accommodate her and the magistrate glossing over inconsistencies got her off the hook. Two of the judges were old fans of hers and all of them hated Victor Sandar and had little or no sympathy for his untimely end.

The witnesses all told the same story, except for the maid who was traumatised and swore that there was another young man present. She insisted this young man shot Rudi Wolfe, the American journalist who had been wounded in the fray. No one else saw this young man and Rudi himself said that Victor Sandar had shot him. No one else saw this young man who the servant said helped her with her shopping, pulled a gun from his jacket and shot Rudi. The French justice system, the police, the magistrates and judges were all only too happy to accept Rudi's version of events, given from his hospital bed while he was making a recovery from the wound the bullet made.

What all the witnesses agreed, and it was a peculiarly uniform story they all told, almost exactly in the same words, was that they were breakfasting together, Alice and Rudi having run away from the asylum where Victor Sandar had tried to incarcerate his daughter because he did not approve of the match and was opposed to Alice having a love affair. Rudi

244

and Cynthia Sandar had rescued her from a fate worse than death. The French loved this. An *affaire de coeur* aroused their sympathy and the media ate it up.

They had taken refuge with the Comtesse de Sevigné, and her past as a film star was grist to the sympathetic mill. That morning, so the story went, they were having breakfast when a demented Victor Sandar had burst in waving a gun and shot Rudi who had tried to stop him.

After this part of the story the statements were very precise. Victor Sandar, presumably deciding to kill the young suitor, his daughter's lover, had lowered the hand holding the gun which Cynthia Sandar swore was his gun and the Comtesse in her wheelchair beside him grabbed it from him, hitting his wrist with her left hand, taking the gun in her right. Victor had bent down to drag Alice Sandar away from the prone body of her love and the Comtesse had propelled herself around the table—she showed them exactly how she had manouevered her chair, taking obvious pleasure in her performance. She had seen Victor put his hands around his daughter's throat and she had thought he was going to kill her. She raised the gun and fired. She had not meant to kill him, simply stop him. She had never fired a gun before in her life.

The authorities accepted this version and Nola herself eventually came to believe it. The powers that be were not about to quibble that

Victor Sandar's fingerprints seemed to be over the Comtesse's instead of hers being over his; they shrugged it away in the face of the rest of the combined statements. They found her guilty of inadvertant manslaughter and gave her the mandatory minimum sentence, suspending it because of her age.

*    *    *

So Nola was able to attend the wedding. Rudi and Alice made a stunning couple and the actress was overcome with emotion.

'It's like a movie,' she cried.

The coverage of the case had brought her to the attention of Malachy Hilton, an Irish film director who was all the rage. His movies were that rare commodity, artistic achievements as well as money-makers. He had a script he wanted badly to shoot. In it an ancient actress was about to be evicted from her home to make room for a motorway. It concentrated on the relationship between her and the lawyer for the construction company. His wife was about to leave him because of his lack of attention to the family; he was pursuing success at the expense of his home life. It told the story of his gradual realisation of how mixed up his priorities were through the eyes of the old actress. Malachy, seeing a close-up of Nola in *Hello!*, decided she would be ideal.

To her amazement she was wooed by him

and signed up for the movie. *The House by the Bridge* starred her and she found herself once more in the limelight; her favourite place to be. She was nominated for an Academy Award and returned to Hollywood at the ripe old age of seventy. They welcomed her with open arms; old scandals now seemed ridiculous. Times had changed. Nola Reine was the flavour of the month. She won her award and that same night, dreaming of the critics' praise, the box office success, the applause and the adulation, she died in her sleep, a smile on her lips.

Cynthia sold the villa to Buck Barrington the Third, who had decided a place in the South of France would hitch him up a notch socially.

Cynthia married one of the doctors from the hospital in Nice, whom she'd met while visiting Rudi there. Together they became involved in a French charity organisation that sent doctors and nurses to trouble spots to back up the Red Cross and bring aid and relief to the suffering. Cynthia took a course in first aid and stayed at her husband's side assisting him. She became plump and her happiness smoothed her face and turned her mouth upwards.

So Victor Sandar's money went to relieve the poor and beleaguered. It was a state of affairs he would not have appreciated. In fact, it would be fair to say that Victor Sandar must be spinning in his grave at all that happened after his death.

Amber Crosbie came to London and at Martin's suggestion—he was quite blunt about it—went into a re-hab clinic. After a year of her being clean and sober they married. They lived with Martin's mother in a little house in the East End of London very peacefully.

Brompton and Angelica Crawley at first fascinated but eventually bored their guests at dinner parties recounting tales of the time when Victor Sandar lived next door, the kidnap, then the murder. The tales became more and more far-fetched and included a naked Alice running around. Everyone who knew Alice realised that was simply not possible.

Rudi and Alice went to live in America. They raised two boys and a girl in a quiet New England town. Cynthia and her doctor visited them regularly but they rarely talked of Victor. They were a close and loving family, appreciating what they had, the happiness won so hardly, the peace and long-lasting joy they had found, the trust and love.

And in her awakening Alice forgot Victor Sandar. He was like a bad dream that sometimes, though seldom recurred and when he intruded in her mind she turned into the arms of the man she loved and he looked upon her with such tenderness and kissed her so softly that she forgot again.

After all, it was far in the past, before she knew what happiness really was.